**"I don't just want you, Anne.
I need you.
We could be so good
for each other."**

He took her hand and let the warm touch of his fingertips lightly stroking her palm plead his case.

She willed her fingers to stop shaking. "I'm sorry, Justin." She felt dazed and numb.

He let her hand lie still in his as he said gently, "He hurt you pretty badly, didn't he? I promise it won't be like that with me."

She turned startled eyes on him. How had he guessed about Chuck? Or was it only a shot in the dark? "What makes you think . . ." she began, but he put a finger to her lips and stopped her.

"I don't think, I know. It's obvious you've been hurt very deeply. I promise you again, it will be different with me. I wouldn't hurt you for the world."

If only she could believe him . . .

Dear Reader:

As the months go by, we continue to receive word from you that SECOND CHANCE AT LOVE romances are providing you with the kind of romantic entertainment you're looking for. In your letters you've voiced enthusiastic support for SECOND CHANCE AT LOVE, you've shared your thoughts on how personally meaningful the books are, and you've suggested ideas and changes for future books. Although we can't always reply to your letters as quickly as we'd like, please be assured that we appreciate your comments. Your thoughts are all-important to us!

We're glad many of you have come to associate SECOND CHANCE AT LOVE books with our butterfly trademark. We think the butterfly is a perfect symbol of the reaffirmation of life and thrilling new love that SECOND CHANCE AT LOVE heroines and heroes find together in each story. We hope you keep asking for the "butterfly books," and that, when you buy one—whether by a favorite author or a talented new writer—you're sure of a good read. You can trust all SECOND CHANCE AT LOVE books to live up to the high standards of romantic fiction you've come to expect.

So happy reading, and keep your letters coming!

With warm wishes,

Ellen Edwards

Ellen Edwards
SECOND CHANCE AT LOVE
The Berkley/Jove Publishing Group
200 Madison Avenue
New York, NY 10016

Second Chance at Love®

MOONLIGHT PERSUASION

SHARON STONE

A SECOND CHANCE AT LOVE BOOK

- 1 -

"NOT TODAY," ANNE HOPKINS said firmly, shaking her head at the cottage cheese and fruit plate her friend Jean Freeman was about to put on Anne's tray. The two women moved through the lunch line at the employees' cafeteria on the third floor of the Dragu Cosmetics Building. As Jean looked on in openmouthed astonishment, Anne heaped her tray with gazpacho, Salade Niçose, whole-wheat bread, a pot of rose-hip tea, a fresh pear, and a generous wedge of blue cheese.

"Anne Hopkins!" Jean exclaimed as they walked toward the cashier. "In the entire five years you've been at Dragu, I don't ever recall your taking a full-course lunch before. You must be celebrating—have you been promoted to head of the marketing division?"

"No, I'm still the most junior of marketing executives." Anne laughed as they seated themselves at their usual table by the windows overlooking Central Park South. "But I have a big meeting at two-thirty, and I'll need all the fortification I can get."

"A big meeting on a Monday? Must be a summons from Dragonescu," Jean said knowingly, using the epithet that their boss, Countess Marie Dragutescu, had

1

acquired early in her career. The flippant nickname had lost none of its suitability as age and success made the founder of the Dragu Cosmetics empire more formidable and imperious than ever.

Anne nodded as she raised a spoonful of the cold soup to her lips. Trepidation increased her appetite rather than taking it away. Besides, she knew it was nearly impossible to gain weight on the streamlined menus the countess insisted that her employees follow to maintain complexions and figures worthy of her beauty emporium.

"Actually, this meal could be my last here, so I may as well enjoy it," Anne explained. She frequently lunched with Jean, who was Dragu's publicity director and had been Anne's mentor when Anne had first come to Dragu as a publicity assistant. The two women had remained close friends since Anne had transferred to the marketing division after acquiring her M.B.A. the previous year.

"Then the countess has read your proposal for the new Marini line?" Jean guessed quickly, opening a container of peach yogurt.

"Apparently," Anne replied, finishing her soup and attacking the large salad. She still wondered at her own temerity in suggesting that the countess collaborate with the daring new Italian designer Mario Marini on a high-fashion line of cosmetics aimed at the growing market of young, affluent, and sophisticated career women. Despite the fact that Anne's market research had shown that very few of the women in this category were buying Dragu Cosmetics, her superiors in the marketing division had tried to discourage her from making her unsolicited presentation to the countess.

"All your arguments are sound," her immediate boss, Al Territo, had conceded several days before. "But you know how touchy the old dame is, Anne. However diplomatically you put it, you're still telling her she doesn't appeal to the young, chic set. What a blow to the ego of a lady who considers herself a living legend! You know the mystique, Anne. The titled but penniless Rumanian refugee who rose from a treatment girl at Elizabeth Arden to become one of the great cosmetics queens in her own right. That's her appeal."

"To women of a certain age—and beyond," Anne agreed. "But that's just it, Al. The mystique cuts no ice with women of my generation. They don't look beyond the image to see that our product line beats the competition's. You know what my survey showed. Women in their twenties and thirties are buying cosmetics labels that match the ones in their clothing—Halston, Dior, Ralph Lauren, Mary Quant. Of course, the established designers don't need the countess—they can bring out their own lines. Marini is brand new on the fashion scene. He's bound to be very hot in a season or two, but right now he wouldn't have the capital to branch out. I'm betting he'll jump at a tie-in with Dragu."

"And Dragonescu will jump, too—right at your throat," Al predicted gloomily.

"I think you're underrating her," Anne said thoughtfully. "The countess expanded from mass-market to more exclusive lines, and she's diversified in other ways when the need has arisen. I think she has the vision to appreciate this opportunity to expand further."

"Okay, go ahead with it." Al shrugged. "It's your head on the chopping block, sweetheart."

Anne had turned in her report on Friday afternoon, and had seen the countess at closing time marching home with it tucked under her arm. First thing this morning, the old woman's secretary, Bessie O'Shea, had buzzed Anne to inform her of the royal summons.

"Couldn't Bessie tell you which way the wind blows?" Jean asked, taking another mouthful of yogurt. Gruff, good-natured, and fearless, Bessie O'Shea had been Marie Dragutescu's secretary for over forty years and was the self-appointed protector and comforter of any employee who excited the old woman's wrath.

"The countess was already closeted in her inner sanctum when Bessie arrived this morning," Anne explained. "She left a memo telling Bessie to inform me of the meeting, and leaving strict orders not to disturb her because she was making a very important call and might be on the phone for some time." Anne knew it wasn't unusual for the countess to put through her own telephone calls on matters she wished to keep mysterious.

"I'm sure your fears are groundless, Anne," Jean said supportively. "You've always been one of Dragonescu's special pets, and she probably loved your report."

"You haven't heard the worst of it," Anne told her. "Bessie buzzed me again at noon to alert me that the countess was bringing my proposal along on her lunch with her attorney, Justin Bradley. Seems he's coming to our powwow as well. Bessie said the countess seemed in good spirits, but then she always is before the kill. Say, isn't Justin Bradley an international lawyer? Maybe he's been called in to arrange for my exile to the Dragu salon in Siberia!"

Both Anne and Jean collapsed laughing. "Honestly, Anne," Jean gasped, "what an imagination. But then, you always were the most creative copywriter in publicity. Justin Bradley," she went on thoughtfully. "What I wouldn't give to meet him—though his meeting you is bound to prove much more fruitful."

"Fruitful?" Anne was puzzled. "You mean if the countess does give me the sack, he can help me get another job?"

"Who's talking about jobs?" Jean said airily. "I mean romance! It's been over a year since Chuck split, hasn't it?"

"A year and a half," Anne said softly, congratulating herself for not wincing at the mention of the man she had lived with for two years. She'd met Chuck in the middle of her first year at Dragu, and the dashing young television executive had swept her off her feet. She'd never met anyone as witty or urbane as Chuck at the small Quaker college she'd attended in Indiana.

It had taken close to a year for Chuck to overcome Anne's straitlaced upbringing and persuade her that living together would be the final confirmation of their compatibility for marriage. She should have known when he hedged about setting a date after that first, almost perfect year together that wedding bells weren't in their future. She should have picked up the signals when he was lukewarm about her going to night school at New York University for her M.B.A. Yet against all reason Anne had clung to the idea of marrying her first love. She wouldn't listen when friends hinted that Chuck wasn't the marrying kind.

In a way she'd been right, Anne thought wryly. Chuck had married, but Anne hadn't been his bride. One night she'd come back to their apartment on East Eighty-fifth Street to find Chuck packing. The following week he'd marched down the aisle with his secretary, whom he'd been seeing all the nights Anne had class or was studying at the library. Anne had been devastated, and the wounds had healed slowly—if, indeed, they were healed even now.

And here was Jean suggesting a romance with Justin Bradley!

"Jeannie," she pleaded, "I know you love to fix people up, but please, not me and Justin Bradley. Look, I've never even seen him."

"Ah, but you're going to," Jean said breezily. "And honey, Justin Bradley doesn't need fixing up. He's one of the most eligible bachelors in town, and I've read that he's particularly partial to redheads. Now, don't tell me you haven't fainted over his pictures in the gossip columns. He's always there with some gorgeous woman or other, including his clients. Especially his clients, I should say, a lot of whom seem to be female. Even our crusty old dragon appears to have succumbed to the Bradley charm. Not many men can get her out of her lair for a lunch date."

"Business lunch," Anne corrected, offering her friend a slice of pear topped with cheese. "And the more you tell me, Jeannie, the more fantastic it seems that you envisage me and this legal lothario as a couple. What would a jet-set glamour boy see in a small town girl like me? Besides, I need another two-timer like I need . . . the salon in Siberia."

Jean shook her head. "Don't be a defeatist, Anne. What Justin would see in you is a willowy redhead with a flawless complexion, eyes like the grotto at Capri, and curves in all the right places. Not to mention brains to match the beauty. And he's been quoted as saying he prefers women who are intelligent and unpretentious. Your ages are in synch, too. You're twenty-seven, and he's in his mid-thirties—the marrying age. As for his reputation, well, Juliet snagged Romeo, didn't she?"

"Yes, and look how that ended," Anne said dryly. Draining her rose-hip tea, she pushed back her chair. "I'm afraid I must leave you to your pineapple juice. I need a moment of silent meditation in my office before the ax falls."

"It's not going to fall," Jean said firmly. "Never mind the pineapple juice. I'll hold your hand as far as the seventh floor."

Anne barely had time for her moment of meditation before her buzzer sounded. It was Bessie.

"They're back early," the secretary reported. "I should have known she wouldn't give him a chance to order dessert on her nickel. But don't worry, she didn't tell me to polish the guillotine, and I've got a hunch the news is good. Anyway, Herself wants you up here pronto."

As Anne rode the elevator one floor to the countess's domain, she asked herself whether her butterflies were inspired by thoughts of Dragonescu or by Jean's intimidating picture of Justin Bradley. Don't be silly, she chided herself, smoothing her gray silk skirt over her long legs, he won't even notice you.

But he did. When Anne entered her employer's plush inner office with its teal damask walls and Venetian chandelier, the most attractive man she had ever laid eyes on was sitting in one of the Louis XV chairs facing the countess's desk. In a movement that bespoke exquisite manners, he rose and looked deeply into her eyes. Anne sensed that courtesy was so ingrained in Justin Bradley that he stood whenever a woman came into his presence; yet the unmistakable admiration with which he watched her cross the room implied a marked interest that was as disconcerting as it was flattering.

Anne was confused less by Justin Bradley's intent gaze than by the way her heart lurched wildly as she returned his appraising look. From Jean's remarks, she had expected him to be handsome. She had even formed a vague picture of him that corresponded in several particulars to the reality. She had anticipated that he would be tall, broadshouldered, and narrow hipped, though she hadn't quite envisaged the air of confident ease that he projected in his well-proportioned six-foot frame. Nor, though she had assumed a top-notch international lawyer would dress with conservative elegance, had she pictured the unique flair with which he wore his perfectly fitted custom-tailored navy suit, patterned designer tie, and impeccably styled shoes. And she hadn't in the least imagined that one look at the man's powerful physique would turn her insides to jelly and set her pulse racing.

What was the matter with her, Anne wondered. She had lived for two years with a strikingly handsome man, and though she had been too upset by the debacle with Chuck to date any of the men who had asked her out since then, those she had turned down without a qualm had included men nearly as good-looking as Justin Bradley. She studied his face, hoping to find the answer to his special magnetism there. His complexion was lighter than she'd imagined, and his light-brown hair waved appealingly over his high forehead, drawing attention to his warm gold-flecked brown eyes. His nose was straight, with slightly flaring nostrils, and his jaw firm, reinforcing his air of patrician elegance. Lips that were full and unmistakably sensual were centered above his somewhat square chin.

Then, as she approached the chair opposite the one by which Justin was standing, he flashed her a dazzling smile, complete with deep dimples and gleaming white teeth, and his whole face suddenly took on a disarmingly boyish cast. With that smile, the debonair playboy had been instantaneously transformed into the boy next door. A very charming, charismatic boy next door, Anne cautioned herself, refusing to be melted by that open, engaging smile, which was strangely like a caress. She wasn't able to prevent her quick intake of breath, but she made her answering smile as distant and impersonal as possible.

"Sit down and catch your breath, Anne. I can't talk to people when they're gulping for air." Countess Marie Dragutescu's brusque greeting penetrated Anne's reverie and increased her confusion. She involuntarily took another deep breath and stood as if rooted to the Aubusson carpet.

With the tact of a born diplomat, Justin Bradley offered Anne a moment to recover by saying suavely, "Let me move your chair to a more comfortable position, Miss Hopkins."

In one swift stride he was by her side. He deftly moved the chair a few inches from its former position so that when he and Anne sat down she found herself looking directly into his eyes. His gaze wandered leisurely over her seated form before returning to her face with an expression that clearly indicated his approval.

Although there was nothing insulting about the man-

ner of his appraisal, he conveyed to Anne that he had
taken in every detail of her appearance, from her wavy
shoulder-length red-gold hair to her slender, demurely
crossed ankles and gray suede pumps. His gaze lingered
appreciatively on her breasts beneath the gray silk blouse
that matched her skirt before following the row of delicate
pearl buttons to where the blouse was tucked in at her
waist.

She was about to thank him for rearranging her chair
when the countess burst into a hearty cackle. "Justin,"
she said good-naturedly, "that was as neat a piece of
sleight of hand as I've ever seen. Not only do you move
Anne's chair so she'll be looking at you instead of at
me, but you move your own chair to the same angle and
even push it closer to hers, all quicker than you can say
Marie Dragutescu—which many people can't say at all.
That's why I had to shorten the name of my firm to
Dragu," she added irrelevantly.

Anne was used to her employer's eccentricities, but
she wondered if she showed the same aplomb in dealing
with them that Justin Bradley exhibited. Seemingly not
the least embarrassed at being caught out in his stratagem,
he gave Anne a look that was both graciously apologetic
and faintly conspiratorial, and then turned to the countess
with his boyishly enchanting smile.

He waited until the old woman's piercing blue eyes
were openly twinkling at him, then said reproachfully,
"Marie, you didn't tell me that your Anne Hopkins was
so stunning."

Though he had addressed the countess, Anne knew
she was intended to be charmed by the compliment. She
vowed not to lose her head. If she'd learned nothing else
from her experience with Chuck, she knew better than
to trust charming men. But even Chuck's calculated al-
lure seemed amateur in comparison with Justin Bradley's
polished gallantry.

"Now, just because I let you call me Marie doesn't

mean you can take liberties with Anne, Justin Bradley," the countess warned gruffly. "Besides, don't you realize the girl won't have ears for your flattery until she's heard whether I'm going to applaud her brainstorm or tell Bessie to bring in the rack and thumbscrews?" Beneath the coronet of white hair and striking black eyebrows, the old woman's imposing features were bathed in merriment. "Forgive me for keeping you in agony, my dear," she said, turning a benevolent gaze on Anne, "but I do enjoy my little moment of suspense."

With a start Anne realized that she had been so bowled over by Justin Bradley that she had almost forgotten that her career was on the line today. With cautious optimism she waited for the countess to continue.

"Even if I didn't think your proposal was brilliant," the now-beaming cosmetics queen went on, "I would still have approved your audacity in approaching me with it. Oh, yes, my dear, I can guess what your colleagues on the tenth floor had to say, all those yes-men in marketing. But I like your idea, Anne. And Justin likes it, too."

Anne was speechless. She knew the countess viewed her as something of a favorite protégée, but *brilliant* was not a word the grande dame used lightly.

"What's even better is that Mario Marini likes it," the countess added, "and I've arranged to send you and Justin off to Rome to hammer out the details with him."

Anne found her voice at last and stammered, "But, Countess, but when—"

"This morning," the old lady interrupted. "Now, stop flustering her with your ogling, Justin. I want Anne to hear every word I say. Where was I? Oh, yes, I called Marini myself, and he was all eagerness and everything that's gracious. Harumph, why shouldn't he be? I put Italy on the map, naming all my early products after the cities there—the Napoli line, the Firenze line, Roma," she said nostalgically.

Anne glanced covertly at Justin Bradley to see if he had taken the countess's reprimand to heart. Evidently he had, for he was now gazing raptly at the old woman with a fondness and an esteem Anne couldn't help approving.

Few people really appreciated the phenomenon that was Marie Dragutescu, and that Justin was apparently one of the few endeared him to Anne against her will. She noticed, too, that Justin's profile was as appealing as the rest of him, showing off to perfection his chiseled nose and the aristocratic planes of his face. But why did her heart have to make flip-flops over this notorious Don Juan, when her every instinct warned her to distrust him? Why did she feel irrationally disappointed that his warm brown eyes were no longer sending her eloquent compliments across the few feet that separated their chairs?

Feeling the countess's shrewd gaze on her, Anne turned her eyes hastily back to her employer. At seventy-two the countess hadn't an ounce of surplus weight on her large-boned frame, and her subtly made-up face had a majesty that dwarfed mere beauty.

Sure of her audience once again, the countess resumed speaking. "Of course, in the old days they all said I was mad," she reminisced fondly. "Americans won't buy what they can't even pronounce, they said. Bosh, I told them. Foreign names have a mystique. You understand, Anne, don't you, my dear? I'm sure Al Territo gave you a rough time over the Marini line. He didn't think my pride could take it, did he? An old nonpareil like me, teaming up with a brash young designer!"

Involuntarily Anne once again stole a glance at Justin, who gave her a conspiratorial wink and another one of his winning smiles. That damned smile of his was unnerving! It created a bond of intimacy between them, and Anne smiled back at him despite herself. Sternly she ordered herself not to look at him again during the meeting.

"Well, I am a nonpareil," the countess was saying, "and I can do what I please. This Marini pleases me—he's innovative, self-made, everything I was at the outset. I know the young women want that sexy male designer image, and they'll buy it. But Anne knows—don't you, my dear?—that it's my magic that will keep them buying, and draw them in droves to my salons for treatments.

"Yes," she concluded, lifting the envelope that contained Anne's proposal from her desk and waving it triumphantly, "this was a stroke of genius. The Marini line! I *like* it!"

"We like it, too, Marie," Justin said smoothly in his rich baritone, compelling Anne to look at him again despite her resolution not to. "But don't you think it's time that Anne and I were properly introduced?"

"It's clear *you* think it's time," the countess said tartly, "and I suppose introductions are in order, seeing that you'll be spending the next few weeks working closely together in Rome. Anne, meet Justin Bradley, our very capable, very expensive lawyer. He knows about law, he knows about negotiating, he even knows about women, I hear." She paused, a wicked gleam in her eye.

"Nevertheless, he doesn't know about cosmetics or designers, and you, my dear, will be acting as my eyes and ears in those departments. It's up to you to decide if Marini knows what he's doing with the shades and the bottles and such, and you're to develop a total marketing plan for the whole shebang. Naturally, everything is subject to my final approval, but you have a great sense of style, Anne, and I have confidence in your judgment."

"Marie, you forgot to complete the introductions," Justin broke in gently.

"Forgot? I never forget a thing." The countess spoke sharply, but the face she turned on Justin was alight with amusement. "Introducing Anne to you just seemed altogether superfluous, Justin. I can see you already take to her as much as I do—though not for the same reasons, I'll wager. Well, Anne has been with me for five years now, and I'll keep her for life as I do all the good ones, so you take care of her for me in Italy. And don't let her fall in love with any of those good-looking Roman gigolos and decide to stay there."

"Will Anne and I be traveling on the same plane?" Justin asked, sounding hopeful.

"No," the countess said tersely. "Not unless you've changed your mind about that detour to Milan to negotiate for your coloratura friend at La Scala. What do they call her? La Tiziana? Bosh! For true titian, her hair doesn't hold a candle to Anne's, and wouldn't even if she used one of my rinses, which she should. Well, never mind. Justin, I want you to get to Milan and conclude that opera business as quickly as possible. How soon can you be in Rome?"

He pursed his lips, and Anne once again noticed the sensual contours of his mouth. She felt a sudden longing to trace those contours with her fingertips; she could almost feel their softness, their velvety texture. What would it be like to be kissed by Justin Bradley? She went all warm and quivery inside at the mere thought of those tantalizing lips on hers, those masterful arms crushing her to that broad chest...

Good Lord! she rebuked herself. If on their first meeting this man evoked such an utterly visceral response in her, what would happen when they were in Rome, perhaps spending hours together every day? The idea of working so closely with Justin Bradley was more than a little overwhelming. She couldn't prevent the tumultuous feelings that recurred every time she looked at him— but she was determined that he should never guess the truth. She must be totally professional, even brusque and aloof, with him. She must convince him that she was immune to his charm, to his entrancing smile, to his overpowering virility.... She forced her mind away from this disturbing groove and concentrated on what he was saying.

"I can leave for Milan tomorrow and wind up my negotiations there in two or three days."

"Good," the countess said. "Anne has a vacation coming up, which you're not going to be able to take in the midst of this Marini campaign, my dear. But I think I can spare a few days for preparations for the trip and rest. Rest is very important for beauty, Anne, so get a lot of it. And do anything else you need to, but don't buy any new clothes. Mario's going to supply you with an entire wardrobe—we discussed it on the phone. From now on you're my Marini girl. And I look forward to seeing you in something more exciting than those tedious grays and beiges you favor, my dear. I don't care what they say about gilding the lily, I want you in bright colors. Marini seems to have produced a few that even God and I hadn't thought of." The old lady chuckled dryly at her own joke.

"Now, if there are no more questions, Anne, you may take the rest of the day off. You won't have a thought for anything but Italy anyway. Make an appointment at the salon for a total treatment on Saturday, and Bessie will book you for a flight next Monday. Justin, why don't you escort Anne to the lobby?"

Clearly there was nothing he would like better. Rising, he gave a slight bow to the countess as she sat behind her massive mahogany desk, which was littered with lotions, blushers, and whatever other samples had been sent up from the lab that day. Marie Dragutescu barely acknowledged Justin's chivalry. She had already buzzed Bessie and was giving the secretary rapid-fire instructions over the phone in her inimitable macaw screech.

Swiftly Justin crossed the antique Aubusson rug with its dusty shades of rose and pastel green and offered Anne his arm.

I won't be snowed by all these courtly gestures of his,

she vowed, and with what she hoped was a polite that-won't-be-necessary look, she rose and preceded him to the outer office.

"My car is downstairs," he murmured as they reached Bessie's desk. "Let me give you a lift home and we can chat a bit. As Marie said, we'll be working very closely together in Rome."

His mouth was so near her ear she could feel his warm breath caress her skin. The way he said "closely" implied that he was thinking of more than a mere working relationship.

He must pull the same number on every woman he meets, Anne warned herself. Even the countess was on to him, and she expected Anne to be on her toes, too. No time like the present to take a businesslike tone with Mr. Justin Bradley.

She halted in front of Bessie's IBM Selectric and gave him a perfunctory smile. "I appreciate the offer," she said coolly, "but I have some details to clear up with Bessie before I leave." She turned a meaningful glance on the countess's secretary, who had been listening to the exchange with undisguised interest.

"Oh, yes," Bessie said, comprehending. "The details. Just got my drilling from Herself." She waved a pink memo paper covered with shorthand.

"I understand," Justin said urbanely, intimating that he understood a lot more than had been spoken. "The pleasure of getting better acquainted awaits us till Rome, then."

"Till Rome," Anne answered weakly, forcing herself to meet his gaze. She soon wished she hadn't, for the long, intimate look he sent her left her more confused than ever. The press of his fingertips against her arm sent an electric thrill through her entire being, and she sighed thankfully when he was gone.

Bessie misinterpreted the sigh. "I don't blame you," she said. "That glance curled my toes and he wasn't even looking at me. Justin Bradley's got his eyes on you, Annie, and believe me, he's choosy."

"I've heard differently," Anne said wryly, a quotation from Browning coming to mind. "'He liked whate'er he looked on,'" she paraphrased, "'and his looks went everywhere.'"

"Well, not everywhere," Bessie drawled, "but I can't deny our Justin's been around. Not that he's any the worse for wear. However, if you're not interested, you're not interested. It should only happen to me." She shrugged philosophically. "All right, kiddo, I think we've allowed enough time for the details. To be honest, they're not complete yet. In the middle of the tirade Herself spied a new shade of nail polish on her desk, and she's going to ring me again after it dries. All I've got so far is that you're taking Alitalia to Rome on Monday, and while your expense account covers new threads from Marini, I'm supposed to check if there's an Italian equivalent of the YWCA."

Anne knew Bessie was kidding. Still, when it came to cash outlays, the countess was eccentric. Her treatment rooms and her own inner sanctum were the epitome of opulence, but she'd been known to fly into a rage over what she considered wasteful use of paper clips and the copying machines. As Bessie succinctly put it, "Herself is a selective spender."

"*Non importa*, Bessie, *non importa*," Anne said, enjoying her first opportunity to try out her college Italian. "In plain English, nothing matters except that I'm going to Rome."

And Justin Bradley will be waiting for you there, an inner demon cautioned. A tremor coursed through her at the thought, and Anne didn't know whether it was due to anxiety or anticipation.

- 2 -

FIFTEEN MINUTES LATER, Anne was happily planning her arrival in the Eternal City as she crossed the lobby of the Dragu Building, heading toward the Fifth Avenue exit.

The voice at her elbow took her by surprise. "I'm glad your details were cleared away so easily," Justin Bradley said, a smile in his deep voice.

He had been waiting for her, she realized, her heart pounding. Or was it just a coincidence?

"I decided to linger on the off-chance," he said smoothly. "You know, Anne, since I'm leaving for Milan tomorrow, it occurs to me that this is our only chance to get together before we join forces in Rome."

"Join forces?" she inquired. "Are we coconspirators? And against whom? I thought the idea was to join forces with Mario Marini." She mustn't let herself be drawn into the easy intimacy Justin was trying to establish between them.

"True," Justin conceded graciously, "but in order to do that, you and I have to synchronize perfectly. Frankly, it would be all to the good if we got to know each other a bit before we get involved with third parties. How about having a drink together . . . and talking?"

17

From a business point of view Justin's proposal made perfect sense. Why, then, Anne wondered, did she suspect him of other than professional motives in suggesting it? It was the way he looked at her, she decided—that interested appraisal he had given her in the countess's office, followed by the veiled invitation now in his smoldering brown eyes. Sexy eyes, Anne thought, and quickly chided herself. Never mind what Justin Bradley had in mind. She could control the situation.

"That's an excellent suggestion, Justin," she said with feigned nonchalance. "Shall we adjourn to the Oak Bar, then?"

"The Oak Bar?" Justin said dubiously. Then meeting her level gaze, he added a shade too quickly, "Sure, why not?"

Anne congratulated herself on her choice of meeting place. The Oak Bar at the Plaza Hotel was a pleasant, convenient, and, above all, businesslike place to chat. In fact, it had once been a males-only preserve for professional conferences, and Justin clearly got the message she had wanted to convey in suggesting it.

Together they left the Dragu Building and walked across the open square outside. As they passed the famous fountain on their way to the Plaza, Anne was conscious of turning heads. She supposed she and Justin made an attractive pair in the eyes of the onlookers, but she reminded herself that they were headed for a business meeting, period. Nevertheless, her heartbeat quickened when he smiled invitingly at her as they walked.

Once ensconced in the dark-paneled Oak Bar, Anne relaxed in her black leather chair facing Justin's and ordered a spritzer of white wine and seltzer.

She was disconcerted when Justin went her one better and ordered plain mineral water. She wondered briefly if they were engaged in a game of one-upmanship, with Justin telling her that if she could keep a cool head by drinking lightly, he could keep a cooler head by not drinking at all. But he met her puzzled look with an easy explanation.

"I have a hard-drinking client from Texas to face at dinner tonight," he said apologetically. "It's mineral water for me now if I want to survive that encounter."

"As you like," Anne replied demurely.

"What I like is being alone with you," he answered in a low voice.

So she hadn't been wrong to mistrust his motives. How obvious could he get? "I'll bet you say that to all your business associates," she said sweetly.

"Touché," he replied easily, raising his hands in mock surrender. "Actually, although I'm used to female clients, you're my first female colleague. Uh-oh." A disarming pretense of panic crossed his finely chiseled features. "Did I say that wrong?"

Anne couldn't help laughing. "On the contrary, you put it very well," she conceded. "A colleague isn't quite the same as a client, is it? And you show yourself quite adaptable to working with a peer of the opposite—ah, gender."

"Why not?" he said. "It's a trend I could learn to enjoy."

"You're not bad company yourself," Anne riposted, "but shall we get down to brass tacks—seeing as you have that hard-drinking Texan to contend with all too shortly?"

"Alas, I do," he assented amiably. "I certainly wish it were otherwise."

There was a definite proposition in the air, Anne realized, both annoyed and excited. She didn't want to examine too closely the mixed emotions Justin Bradley aroused in her, and she led the conversation back to safer ground.

"Tell me, Justin," she said equably, "just how do you see your role in the Mario Marini acquisition?"

He cocked his head pensively. "Marini is young, imaginative, and probably on the verge of becoming an international fashion superstar. A New York connection would be very useful to him just now, and we can offer him that. On the other hand, we want to be sure we're going with a winner. Now, my job is to draw up the contracts with Marini's lawyer, to establish who gets what for how much. But as we proceed with the negotiations, it wouldn't hurt to keep our options open in case Marini proves a mere flash in the pan. His showing of his fall collection in three weeks is the key. We've got to have the contracts ready by then. If the collection's a hit, we'll dot the *i*'s and cross the *t*'s as the flashbulbs are popping. But if it's a flop—well, we've left ourselves a graceful out."

Anne shifted uneasily in her chair. "I see. You're going to try to postpone the final signing until we know we've got a sure thing. But I wouldn't have suggested the Marini tie-in unless I believed in it."

At that moment their drinks arrived, giving Justin some pause for thought. "I read your report very carefully," he said finally, "and found it pretty sharp. Naturally Marie wouldn't be sending us both off to Rome unless the Marini deal looked promising. When they spoke this morning, she and Marini agreed to agree, and we're going over there in complete good faith. But the very qualities that have helped Marini rise so quickly— his spirit of innovation and creativity—could kill him faster than you can say, '*Ciao*, Mario.' I'm just saying we have to hedge our bets against a possible disaster."

"I don't feel too comfortable with that," Anne admitted, taking a long sip of her spritzer.

"Aha," Justin said. "Do I detect a small-town girl of upright principles here?"

Anne flushed. "I grew up in Richmond, Indiana, and my parents are Quakers," she admitted, "but I don't think I'm being overscrupulous—do you?"

"You're being scrupulous," he hedged, "and I respect

that. If it's any comfort to you, Marini's lawyer is one of the shrewdest in Italy, and I'm sure they know our game. They have confidence in his designs, so they don't mind waiting a bit for the contracts to be signed. They just want the signatures there as soon as the collection is shown—for maximum publicity, you understand."

"Yes," Anne replied, taking another sip of her spritzer. "I started out in the publicity department at Dragu, you know."

"No, I didn't know," Justin said in an intimate drawl. "There's a lot I don't know about you, which is why I suggested we get together and talk."

"There's a lot I don't know about you, either," she challenged.

They looked at each other then, a long, appraising look. If only he weren't so blasted handsome, Anne thought. She longed to run her hands through his wavy biscuit-colored hair, to press her fingers in the dimples on either side of his smile. She had vowed to keep this meeting strictly professional, yet when he looked at her with those melting golden-brown eyes, she felt herself dissolve with longing. But Chuck had made her feel that way at the beginning, and look what had come of it.

"I'll tell you whatever you want to know," Justin answered her. "For starters, I'm a New Yorker. My father was a lawyer, but the criminal kind, and I've always wanted to be a lawyer, but not the criminal kind."

She liked his directness. "And why not the criminal kind?" she prodded.

He showed his dimples. "Guess I've got my own scruples. To my dad the courtroom show was all. He didn't particularly care whether a client was guilty or innocent as long as *he* looked good before the jury. That's not my style—I like everyone to look good. I'm an arbitrator rather than a grandstander, I suppose."

"Still, you must find international law exciting," Anne suggested.

"Sure it's exciting. But for me the real satisfaction comes when people on opposite sides of the globe get together for the benefit of both parties. I just provide the glue that binds them," he said modestly. "And how about you?" he continued. "How did a Quaker from Richmond, Indiana, get into the unlikely field of cosmetics?"

Anne tried not to bristle. "I guess it does seem strange for someone with my background to end up in the cosmetics business," she acknowledged. "When I was an undergraduate at Earlham College, one of my English professors—who was not a Quaker," she conceded with a twinkle in her eye, "suggested I had a flair for writing and might find my métier in publicity. He advised me to contact the New York agencies—I must have communicated a certain restlessness. Anyway, a personnel firm got me an entry-level job in the publicity department at Dragu. Like you, I enjoy helping people feel good about themselves. I saw that the countess really cared about making women beautiful and confident, and I believe in her products. I use them myself."

Justin drained his glass before responding. "Cosmetics or no, you're a very beautiful woman, Anne. A very beautiful woman," he repeated softly, almost reverently.

Anne felt a warm glow radiate through her. It didn't sound like a line. There was nothing lascivious in his voice or in the near-worshipful way he looked at her. Yet his seeming sincerity might simply be the secret of his technique.

"Would you like another spritzer?" he offered, as if to spare her the embarrassment of acknowledging his tribute.

"No, thank you. One drink's my limit," Anne said, wishing she didn't sound so prim.

"One drink?" He quirked an eyebrow at her. "One double vodka martini I could understand, but that spritzer can hardly have gone to your head," he teased.

Anne found herself smiling at him. "I'm afraid I'm

betraying my teetotaling origins. Believe me, my parents would be shocked even at the one spritzer. They never drink anything stronger than lemonade or iced tea."

"Ah, but that's in Richmond, Indiana," Justin said. "I hope when we get to Rome you'll unbend to the extent of sharing a bottle of Orvieto or Verdicchio with me over dinner. Of course, we could ask for some 'seltz' on the side if you're addicted to spritzers, but it seems a pity to adulterate a fine wine."

"I wouldn't dream of it," Anne demurred. "As they say, 'When in Rome...'" The words were out of her mouth before she realized that she had tacitly assented to letting Justin wine and dine her in Italy.

"I'm glad you're flexible," he said easily. "And you have a certain old-fashioned quality that's refreshing. It seems a cliché to talk about the all-American girl, but I'll bet you were a cheerleader in high school."

The unexpected statement and the teasing glint in Justin's eyes made Anne laugh. "Cheerleader and aquaette," she admitted.

"What on earth is an aquaette?"

Anne laughed again at his look of utter bewilderment. "Synchronized swimming," she explained. When Justin still looked at her blankly, she elaborated. "It's similar to water ballet. You remember Esther Williams? Anyway, we choreographed routines—that's what the individual water ballets are called—around a general theme, made our own costumes, decorated the swimming pool area, and gave a big show at the end of the year. It was lots of fun really."

"I can see you enjoyed it—your eyes are sparkling. What kind of themes did you use?"

"The theme was based on the music. One year we did *Camelot*—not the greatest choice, because our tinfoil crowns were in danger of floating away from our heads every time we did one of the more elaborate stunts. Between acts we kept sending the coach out for bobby pins. My senior year we did *Swan Lake*—that was probably our best show. Another time the theme was *West Side Story*."

"Did girls dance—I mean, swim—the male parts?" Justin asked.

"Oh, no, the aquaettes were coed," Anne told him. "We recruited from the boys' swim team."

"Hm. I was on the swim team at the Dalton School," Justin mused. "Could you see me as an aquaette?"

"Sure, if you have the legs for it," Anne quipped. A mental picture of Justin in bathing trunks made her heart race. "Had you been available, you would have been a perfect Lancelot for our *Camelot*."

"And were you Guinevere?" he asked in a low voice.

"I was,". she admitted, suddenly embarrassed. She took another sip of her spritzer.

"I thought so," he said, his eyes dancing. "You do have something of a regal air, you know."

Anne made a face. "I thought you said I was the all-American girl."

"That, too," he replied. "But where's the contradiction? Head cheerleader, homecoming queen, Guinevere in the aquaettes..."

"I was *not* head cheerleader," Anne protested.

"No? But I'll bet you were editor of the literary magazine."

"Really!" Anne laughed. "Now I suppose you'll claim to be clairvoyant."

"*You* tell *me* what I am," he said seductively. "I've told you some of my impressions of you. It's your turn now."

"Well," Anne began, agreeing to his game, "I'll bet you can sing. You have a very rich speaking voice, and the countess mentioned your negotiations at La Scala, so I suppose you're musically inclined."

He laughed. "You make it sound as if I'm negotiating a singing contract for myself. I do confess that I've fantasized myself as an operatic hero occasionally, but bass-baritone never won fair lady in any opera I've ever seen."

"But you do sing?" Anne persisted.

"In the shower," he joked. "Actually, you're very perceptive. I did study voice as a teenager, and I even appeared in the chorus at the Met a few times when they needed extras for *Aïda* and *Boris Godounov*."

"Really? I may have heard you, then. My mother always tuned in the Texaco opera broadcasts every Saturday, and I used to listen with her. I can still hear Milton Cross saying, 'And now, live from the Metropolitan Opera in New York City . . .' and describing the great gold curtain going up."

"You like opera, then?" Justin's eyes lit up with enthusiasm. "If only I were free tonight. They're doing a magnificent *Madama Butterfly* at the Met. I've seen it twice already."

"You really are an opera buff!" Anne exclaimed. "And you must have nerves of steel. *Butterfly* has to be one of the saddest stories . . . I can't contemplate watching that poor, forsaken bride go through all that agony three times in one season."

"So you have a sentimental side," he said, caressing her with his eyes in a way that made her heart ache with an undefined longing.

She never got to answer the question in Justin's gaze, for at that moment a woman's voice rang out loudly over the low monotone of the elegant bar.

"So there you are, Justin, honey." Striding toward their table was a stunning amazon of a woman, her hair similar in hue to Anne's except that the color had clearly come out of a bottle. Her tall body was draped in a full-length sable coat, beneath which Anne saw dark-brown lizard boots.

"Justin honey," the woman continued, still some distance from their table, "why didn't you tell me you wanted a little drink or two before our dinner?" The Western twang in her voice shouted Texas to Anne's ears.

Justin rose and said easily, "Hello, Linda Beth, this is Anne Hopkins. Anne's a business associate," he added—unnecessarily, Anne thought. She also thought the kisses he planted on Linda Beth's cheeks in the European style lasted longer than necessary.

"Well, aren't you a pretty little thing for a business associate," Linda Beth said dismissively. She turned her full attention to Justin immediately. "Justin, darlin', why don't we just mosey on up to my suite and start the evening out right?"

"Justin's promised me a lift home," Anne was startled to hear herself say. "And we haven't finished our conversation yet, either."

"That's right, honey"—Linda Beth remained unruffled—"you fight for your man, hear?" She put a hand on Justin's shoulder. "Just don't make him late for dinner." Linda Beth's eyes found Justin's and they exchanged a mutual wink. "See you later, sugar pie." With a negligent wave she moved off.

"So that's your hard-drinking client from Texas. Now, why did I get the impression the client would be a red-faced, overweight cowboy?" Anne asked with feigned innocence.

"You were thinking of an Oklahoman, I suppose," he answered, straight-faced.

They both laughed at once, yet Anne's inner demon was sounding the alarm louder than ever.

Justin stopped laughing and looked deeply into her eyes. "Anne . . ."

"Please," she interrupted, "let's keep this on a business-associate level." Seeing Justin flirt with Linda Beth had once more put Anne on her guard.

"I thought we were getting to know one another," he said with a hint of reproach. "And we seemed to be getting on famously until Linda Beth's—ah, interruption. Actually, I'd like to hear more about your all-American girlhood out in Indiana. While you're finishing your drink, you can tell me about it. Then I'll give you that ride home I offered."

"You won't be too late for Linda Beth?" Anne couldn't resist asking.

He smiled. "No one's ever too late for Linda Beth. Tell me about yourself."

Justin was easy to talk to, and Anne found herself telling him about growing up an only child on her parents' farm on the outskirts of Richmond, her scholarship to Earlham, and her quest for something more in life than a house to clean and children to raise. "Though I do want to get married and have children. It's just that I know I can do more. I want to go out in the world. I always have."

"I know what you mean," he said. "You're a doer, an achiever, Anne. So am I. We seem to have a lot in common." He gave her another of his meaningful looks.

Anne reined herself in. She had been going on so about herself that she hadn't really given him a chance to reciprocate. Or, she thought suddenly, was this a tactic of his? He was a clever lawyer. She had revealed a great deal of herself, but she still knew no more of him than he had disclosed before the arrival of Linda Beth.

It was depressing to realize the extent of the legacy of suspicion Chuck had left her with. Anne felt a momentary confusion and downed the last of her spritzer to cover it.

"Come on," Justin said, rising. He took her hand, his fingers warm and strong over hers. There was a quick pressure and a slight caress before he released her. A tingling glow sped through her at the touch.

Justin led her into the ornate gold-and-white lobby of the Plaza and through the revolving door to the front of the hotel.

"I'm parked in a garage a few blocks away," he said. "Why don't you wait here, and I'll be back for you in a jiffy."

"Sounds good," Anne said, glad for the brief respite from his magnetic presence. As Justin loped away, she asked herself if he was really as taken with her as he seemed, or if it was all an act.

His interest was unmistakable, but the nature of that interest disturbed her. She mustn't mistake lust for genuine feeling, and she had no reason to believe Justin wanted anything more than to add her to his list of conquests. If only she didn't find him so devilishly attractive.

And if only his manners weren't so etiquette-book perfect, she thought, as amid heavy traffic a gleaming silver Porsche darted into a temporary parking place. Justin emerged from the driver's seat to hold the door for her on the passenger side.

"Your address, ma'am?" he asked lightly once he'd returned to the driver's seat and put the gearshift into drive.

"East Eighty-fifth Street, between First and Second," she told him.

"Oh, Yorktown?" he said conversationally. "There are some terrific Hungarian restaurants up there."

"Yes, there are," Anne said quietly, recalling with a stab of pain the romantic evenings she and Chuck had spent in some of them.

As they headed uptown, Anne noticed how easily Justin handled the foreign sports car. His long fingers moved deftly from the steering wheel to the gearshift as he glided the Porsche through the rush-hour traffic, dodging taxis and buses and seeming to time his arrival at all the lights just as they turned green.

"I suppose you must wonder about Linda Beth's— ah, familiarity," he remarked casually as he turned left onto First Avenue.

Anne saw the half smile that lurked in the corners of his lips as he waited for her response. "Your private life is none of my business," she said coldly.

"Business, business." He gave an exaggerated sigh. "Are you *all* business, Anne Hopkins?"

"*My* private life is none of *your* concern," she snapped.

"And here I thought we'd agreed I'd be the perfect Lancelot to your Guinevere," he teased, humming the opening bars of "If Ever I Would Leave You" in a melodious baritone. When that failed to coax a smile from her, his tone became serious. "Anne, all I'm asking is a chance to get to know you. Is that too much to ask?"

She felt confused; he sounded so sincere.

"No, but—"

"Good. Then let's keep our options open. Now, about Linda Beth—"

"Justin, you don't owe me any explanations."

"Then you do think there's something to explain?"

"I'm told your picture appears regularly in the gossip columns," Anne said, "and that there's usually a gorgeous woman or two with you."

"Safety in numbers," he joked.

"Oh?" she asked, skeptical.

"I suppose you think I eat it all up—being photographed with glamorous women."

"Not at all," Anne said dryly. "I'm sure you find it a loathsome duty—but after all, you have to humor your female clientele."

"If you really want to know, I do find the invasion of my privacy distasteful," he said sincerely. "Look, I don't pretend to have led a monkish life." When Anne remained silent, he went on. "I'll admit I like female companionship and enjoy a certain—ah, rapport with some of my women clients. And what I do in my personal life doesn't affect my business life. But they know and I know that it doesn't mean anything."

"I see," Anne said coolly. "And what would you do if one day a client happened to misunderstand this . . . rapport of yours?"

"You don't understand," he said brusquely. "Look," he continued more gently, "what I'm trying to say is, I don't start it. I'm not the kind of creep who leads women on. They set the tone, not me. And I make sure it never gets to the point of misunderstanding. But there's always a certain sexual awareness in any relationship between a man and a woman. Don't you agree? Don't you feel it between us?" he asked in a low voice.

"You're about to pass my building," Anne dodged, bracing herself as Justin pulled the Porsche to a sudden halt.

"You haven't answered my question," he persisted quietly, insistently, facing her across the bucket seats.

"No, and I don't think I will," she replied as she unfastened her seat belt. "As you said, we'll be joining forces in Rome. I'll reserve judgment until I get to know you better. Frankly, Justin, you're moving too fast for me."

"You have the wrong idea about me," he pleaded with warm brown eyes. "But if you'll let me I'll change your mind."

He leaned forward, and she thought he was going to kiss her, and her heart pounded wildly. But instead, he took her hand and raised it to his lips. The moist imprint of his open mouth on her palm proved more unsettling than the passionate attack she'd been prepared to forestall.

"*Arrivederci*, Anne, *carissima*," he said softly as he released her hand at last with a final, thrilling pressure. She hoped he didn't suspect she understood the Italian endearment as she sprang from the car with only a "Mona Lisa" smile of farewell.

- 3 -

ANNE LOVED THE Hotel Raphael at first sight. Good old Bessie, she thought as the taxi pulled up before the ivy-covered terra-cotta residence, which was nestled in one of the most venerable and picturesque sections of Rome. But perhaps she didn't owe her accommodations to Bessie after all, Anne reflected as she followed the porter into the bold ultramodern interior. The stark white sculptured walls of the lobby alternated with sheets of plate glass, and couches stood amid antique statues and ornate plants on colorful Oriental rugs. Apparently the countess was capable of largess when it suited her purposes. She had no doubt selected the hotel herself.

When Anne gave her name to the desk clerk, he broke into a delighted smile. "*Sí*, Signorina Hopkins, we have been expecting you," he said. "And so has a certain gentleman."

Anne's pulses quickened as she remembered the countess's admonition to Justin to take care of her in Italy. He'd seemed only too willing to do just that, and, recalling their parting in the Porsche, Anne felt a frisson of longing flow through her. In eager anticipation she scanned the lobby for Justin's boyish face.

He wasn't there. As if divining her puzzlement, the desk clerk elaborated. "Signor Mario Marini is waiting for you on the sofa to your left," he explained in a low voice.

Anne followed his gaze. The dark Italian the desk clerk indicated was about Justin's height, but there the resemblance ended. Mario Marini was not handsome, though he projected an attractive masculine presence. Perhaps, too, he was psychic, for at that moment he gazed toward the counter where Anne was standing with her luggage, and his eyes lit up as if in recognition.

In a twinkling he was by her side confirming her identity as his monkeylike face split in a grin that made him instantly likable. "*Piacere*," he crooned. "You're every inch the remarkable redhead the contessa described. But you seem surprised to see me, *non è ver'*? You were expecting Signor Justin Bradley. *Sì*, I know all about it. Signor Bradley is just now with my attorney, Maestro Olivetti. The maestro did not think it was an opportune moment for Signor Bradley to leave, so he suggested I come to meet you instead. You are not displeased, I hope? *Eccellènte*! Come, I escort you to your room."

Later, steamy and relaxed as she stepped from the tub in the modern black-tiled bathroom of her suite, Anne thought about Mario and realized that she had found a friend. After the instant turmoil Justin had thrown her into, it was a relief to develop an easy rapport with an eligible bachelor of her own age without any sexual undercurrents on either part. For though Mario had been all attentiveness, Anne sensed that he appreciated her as he might an exquisite *objet d'art,* and her intuition told her that his affections were engaged elsewhere. Nevertheless, he was appropriately solicitous and upon learning that she had no plans for her first evening in Rome, he had suggested that they dine together.

"A woman *sola* in a Roman trattoria"—he'd shaken his head in consternation—"is open, shall we say, to misconstruction. Even the hotel dining room . . . and besides, it is not at a hotel that one samples the delights of our Roman cuisine. No, I will take you," he said, settling the matter. "You would like a nap now. I will return at nine and we'll go out for a light supper. Then early to bed for you," he had said without innuendo, "and tomorrow you will come to my salon."

Just as she was drifting into sleep a few minutes later, Anne heard the insistent ring of her bedside phone. *"Pronto,"* she answered sleepily, thinking that it must have been her phone she'd heard earlier when she was in the tub. There had been a faint ringing, but at that distance she couldn't tell whether the sound came from her room or one of the adjoining ones, and she'd been too luxuriantly comfortable to go find out.

"Anne, you're there at last." Even in her sleepy state, she recognized the friendly baritone as Justin's.

"I'm here," she said foggily. "Hello, Justin."

"Hello, Anne. Welcome to Rome." Even on the telephone his voice conveyed unspoken depths. "Look, I'm sorry about not being able to make it this afternoon—"

"Doesn't matter." She yawned. "Mario came. I'm having dinner with him at nine," she explained, "so I thought I'd get in a little nap in the meantime." Despite his insinuating tone, Justin didn't affect her so much over the telephone. Or perhaps it was because she was half-asleep. She'd have to remember that.

The silence on the other end of the receiver seemed interminable. Finally she heard him say curtly, "Mario? I see, very nice."

"Yes, he is very nice," she said sleepily.

"I'm glad you think so," Justin replied shortly. "Well, I'll let you get your beauty sleep, then. I know how Marie believes in it. Shall I call you in the morning?"

"Mmmm, yes. The morning," said Anne, thinking

how good it would be to have a full night's sleep in this soft, comfortable bed.

It was after eight when she awoke again. She only vaguely remembered Justin's call. Maybe she'd dreamed it. She didn't think so, but she couldn't recall exactly what 'hey'd said to each other. She hoped she hadn't sounded totally incoherent. Well, Justin should understand about jet lag—he must have it often enough with his job. She had better stop thinking about him for the moment, and get dressed for her supper with Mario.

When he rose from the sofa to greet her as she crossed the lobby, Mario was all eyes. But his gaze was not for her, Anne realized quickly, but for her ensemble. Moreover his expression was anything but approving.

"A perfect outfit—for an audience with the Holy Father." He dismissed her pale lavender velvet dress with its flared skirt and bolero jacket. "And that color, it washes you out."

"Washes me out?" Anne echoed miserably. She knew his remarks were purposely exaggerated, yet his disapproval was all too real. His frown accentuated his simian features, reminding Anne of a disgruntled old ape.

But as he examined her further, his face cleared. "The lines, at least, are good," he admitted grudgingly. "And the navy traveling suit you wore this afternoon had a certain chic, if not the elegance of a Mario Marini," he amended with a smile. "But you have the conservative instincts. It is disappointing. Perhaps there are those who would admire your Botticellian modesty, but me, I prefer a touch of the flamboyant."

She could have guessed that from his own attire. His crushable cotton open neck shirt in neon red was the perfect foil for his lightweight cotton suit. Mario took in her admiring gaze and smiled. "It's my own design," he said. "I am planning a new line of men's clothing. All comfort, all wonderful color. What do you think?"

"I think you're a true artist," she said graciously,

accepting the arm he offered and following him through the hotel's double doors. "But save some of your wonderful colors for me," she teased as he helped her into a taxi. "The countess seems to think I need them. And from what you said earlier, I gather you agree."

"I know exactly the colors that will suit you," he assured her confidently. "When you visit my salon tomorrow, you will see for yourself. But now we are on our way to the Sans Souci." In rapid Italian he directed the taxi driver, who shot off at breakneck speed.

When they reached the Via Veneto, Mario pointed out to her that this was Rome's main thoroughfare. But in the dark Anne could see very little of its fashionable boutiques and busy cafés. Then the cabdriver turned onto the narrow Via Sicilia and pulled up before the posh Sans Souci restaurant.

Anne had a sense of *déjà vu* as they descended the thickly carpeted stairs to the dimly lit mirrored bar below street level. Suddenly it hit her—of course, it was right out of the Fellini classic *La Dolce Vita*. She half-expected to see a blasé Marcello Mastroianni among the cosmopolitan-looking men and tastefully bejeweled women who crowded the bar and the restaurant behind it. All the patrons seemed to be enjoying themselves enormously. Light laughter and a soft babble of conversation filled the rooms attractively. Waiters dashed to and fro or hovered solicitously. Flambéed creations erupted off and on at almost every table. The restaurant seemed to love its indulgence in culinary fireworks.

"We order first, then go to our table," Mario explained as the maître d' handed her a large menu. Mario was obviously well known to the man, and they exchanged pleasantries as Anne studied the impressive list of classical Italian dishes and international specialties.

"I'm a bit overwhelmed," she told Mario. "Perhaps you'd better order for me."

"*Certamente,*" he agreed solicitously. "The *espadon*

is particularly good here. That is a mixed grill served with a rice pilaf and topped with a marvelous green peppercorn sauce."

"Sounds divine," Anne said, feeling adventurous.

"*Benissimo.* I will tell the maître d' we have decided, and we can have a drink at our table. It is too noisy here for us to become properly acquainted."

They were whisked to a table in the center of the carnivallike atmosphere of the dining room. Anne followed Mario's lead in ordering Campari and soda as a predinner drink. As they sipped their apéritifs, Mario chattered away nonstop about his boyhood in Naples learning the tailoring trade from his father, and how he'd always dreamed of becoming a celebrated designer with a salon in Rome.

As she listened to his monologue, Anne let her eyes roam idly over to the crowded bar. With a start she recognized a familiar profile in the entryway to the dining room.

Justin! Even across a crowded room he seemed to cast a seductive spell on her. As she surveyed his lean, muscular physique, clad in a striking black suit with white shirt and black tie, she was suddenly conscious of her own body, and a yearning greater than she had ever known filled her every pore. Her breasts seemed to grow fuller and were pervaded by an erotic tingling, while a warm, womanly glow radiated through her. When at last the sensation had run its course, she was left feeling weak and tremulous.

From their first meeting in the countess's office, she had found Justin disturbing, but she had attributed her agitation to his own unconcealed attraction to her, and the suggestive way he looked at and spoke to her. Now she realized with alarm that even his mere physical presence affected her more powerfully than had anything in her experience.

Justin seemed to be waiting for someone. He gave an

impatient glance at his watch, then turned as if expecting
a companion to emerge from the area beyond the bar,
where Anne guessed the rest rooms were located.

He must be dining with Maestro Olivetti. Had he
mentioned it when he'd called? She didn't remember.
But Mario had indicated that the two lawyers had been
involved in a long session today, and it was very likely
that, if the negotiations had been difficult and protracted,
Justin might have suggested a meal together to relax the
tensions. Or the proposal might have come from Olivetti.
In any case, what a coincidence that they had come to
the Sans Souci. As soon as Justin was joined by the
maestro, she would try to catch their attention and the
four of them could spend the evening together. Justin
would no doubt offer to see her home...

"But I am boring you with all this talk about myself,"
Mario said suddenly, as if aware of her distraction. "Ah,
here comes the insalata—I have ordered a special salad
composed of many kinds of truffles."

"It looks delicious," Anne replied, but after a brief
glance at the concoction of exotic food, she returned
her gaze to Justin. She had just lifted a forkful of the
salad to her lips when he was joined by his dinner companion. But the person who took his arm and smiled up
at him as the maître d' led them into the dining room
was clearly not Maestro Olivetti. On the contrary, she
was one of the most breathtakingly beautiful women Anne
had ever seen. As they walked together, she and Justin
seemed to be chatting easily, as if they were intimately
acquainted.

If Justin had ever had a preference for redheads, this
raven-haired paragon would alter that, Anne thought miserably. Her simply dressed black hair was the perfect
frame for her classic features, and she carried her lithe,
long-waisted body with the grace of a flamingo. And her
dress! A startling shade of red, somewhere between ruby
and vermilion, it had been cut in such a way that when-

ever its wearer moved, flashes of red sequins glittered amid the silk crepe. When she was still, the smooth red crepe reclaimed its own. It was a masterful design. Somehow it was the more galling to Anne that Justin's date should be swathed in a shade she knew would clash horribly with her own flame-colored hair.

The more she stared at the woman's dress, the more the color seemed vaguely familiar; yet where could she have seen such a blinding hue before? Of course! Mario's shirt! Quickly Anne shifted her gaze to check. "Ah, you've returned from whatever far country your thoughts had traveled to," she heard him say. "But why are you staring at my chest?"

Anne was mortified. "Forgive me, Mario. I just happened to notice a woman in a dress that seems to match your shirt . . ."

At her words Mario's head turned quickly. Just as swiftly he turned back to face Anne.

"Her escort is Justin Bradley, my—ah, business associate," she said, "but I've never seen the woman before."

"I, on the contrary, have seen her many times," Mario said, his voice faintly ironic. "Her name is Monica Arletti, and she's my . . . my best model."

That explained the dress. But it didn't explain why Justin should be dining with her, unless perhaps he and Maestro Olivetti had gone to the salon today and Justin had struck up an acquaintance with the stunning model. Quick work, Anne thought bitterly. But then, Justin had already shown himself to be a fast mover with women.

The maître d' was leading them in the direction of the table she shared with Mario, Anne realized with a wild flutter in her stomach. Just then Justin spotted her, and their eyes locked. She thought she saw his jaw muscles tighten. He said something to Monica, then to the maître d'.

"I think they're coming over to our table to say hello,"

she told Mario, hoping her voice didn't betray her consternation. She pushed her long red-gold curtain of hair over one shoulder in a nervous gesture.

"Oh, really?" Mario said casually, capturing her hand as she was about to return it to her lap. "But what's this? Anne, that nail lacquer—it is one of the countess's products, of course?"

"Of course," Anne said mechanically, conscious that Justin and Monica were only a few feet away now. "Why? Is there anything wrong?" She had applied the nail polish on the plane and thought she might have smudged it.

"Not at all. I am just so taken by the color," Mario said, bringing her hand closer to his face. "Just the right blend of pink and purple—the tint of a rose from the Garden of Eden!" He lowered her hand to the table again, but kept it clasped tightly in his own. "Your countess's instincts are just like mine. I can see our ideas will accord perfectly."

"What's this about according perfectly? No, forgive me, I won't interrupt your private joke." It was Justin's voice, yet so colorless and bland that Anne might not have recognized it.

"Good evening, Justin," she said lamely. His nearness was all too disconcerting, and she felt her hand quiver in Mario's.

"Good evening, Anne," Justin echoed neutrally. "May I present Monica Arletti?"

"*Piacere,*" Anne mumbled, looking into the model's lambent emerald eyes.

"Same here. Hi."

"You're American!" Anne exclaimed.

"Sure. Italian-American actually. Third generation. *Ciao,* Mario," the model acknowledged her employer.

Though Monica's speech was informal, her tone was unfriendly, and Anne wondered at its barely veiled hostility until she realized the anger was all for Mario. She could almost see the sparks ignite in their eyes when

Mario returned Monica's salutation with stony civility. Perhaps he was a difficult man to work for. Yet it was hard to picture Mario in the role of Simon Legree. Maybe Monica was temperamental. But Mario had referred to her as his best model.

"Well, small world, isn't it?" Justin said tightly. "We all meet at the Sans Souci, and I must say you two seem as if you haven't a care in the world."

"Quite true," Mario replied easily. "This evening is one of the most pleasant I've ever spent." Then, turning to Anne with marked cordiality, he added, "And I hope there will be many more like it, Anne."

"I don't see why not, Mario," she murmured. "After all, we are going to be partners." She was grateful to him for sensing that this was an awkward moment for her, and his warmth was welcome in the face of Justin's stiff formality. No doubt Justin was uncomfortable at being caught out with a glamorous date. Monica certainly wasn't his client, so what could she be to him except a woman he hoped to sleep with—or perhaps already had?

As if to confirm her suspicions, he slid his arm around the model's slim waist. Anne was vaguely aware that Mario was running his fingertips lightly over the back of her hand, but there was something impersonal about the caress. Or maybe it was just that she didn't feel attracted to him.

Monica, however, seemed all too responsive to Justin's touch. Sliding into the crook of his arm, she purred, "Justin, I don't think the captain will hold our table forever."

"Don't let us keep you," Mario said, all affability. "Anne and I can easily pick up where we left off."

"I'll bet you can," Justin said shortly, and wheeled, Monica in tow, heading for a distant area of the dining room.

"They didn't even say good-bye," Anne commented

dazedly as she watched Justin and Monica retreat toward a darkened corner of the restaurant.

"My fault, I think," Mario apologized. "I doubt that either one of them was pleased to see me. You see, Monica Arletti promised to marry me three weeks ago. Then she went home for a visit and looked up her old childhood friend, Mr. Justin Bradley."

- 4 -

ANNE AWOKE THE next morning with a strange sense of dislocation. For a moment she gazed at the unfamiliar appointments of her bedroom and thought she must still be dreaming. Sitting up in bed, she blinked at the onslaught of lemony Roman sunshine pouring in through the gauzy white curtains. Then she remembered.

"Italy," she mumbled to herself. "Mario. Justin."

Justin! Their encounter of the previous evening came back to her with sickening clarity. No doubt he was just now awakening with Monica at his side. Anne glanced at her bedside traveling clock. Ten o'clock! She had set the alarm for eight-thirty, but had apparently turned it off in mid-ring and gone back to sleep.

So Monica had probably gone to the salon already, and Justin . . . ? Why did she have the impression he was supposed to call her this morning? Perhaps he had mentioned it in that half-remembered phone call that had interrupted her nap. But would he honor that commitment after last night?

When Anne and Mario had left the restaurant, Justin and Monica were still sitting at their table in the shadowed alcove. Anne couldn't tell whether the other couple noticed them leaving, but they certainly hadn't acknowledged her and Mario's departure in any way.

She still wasn't sure why Justin had seemed so out of sorts. She might have attributed it to jealousy, but the idea of Justin being jealous of Mario seemed ludicrous, especially with the ravishing Monica Arletti clinging to his side.

No, Anne decided, jealousy didn't account for Justin's peculiar behavior at the Sans Souci. She had told him on the phone that she would be having supper with Mario—that much she did recall—and what could be more natural since Mario was the reason she was in Rome in the first place? Most likely Justin had merely been chagrined at having Anne see him with Monica, especially if he was still as intent on adding Anne to his list of conquests as he had seemed in New York.

Despite Mario's gloomy forecast that Monica would soon be announcing her engagement to Justin instead of to himself, Anne thought it more likely that Monica, too, was a mere addition to Justin's long line of romantic entanglements. He must be thirty-five or thirty-six, and she had observed that most men who remained bachelors by that age were committed to the unmarried state—though not to celibacy by any means.

So Justin's intentions toward herself could not be honorable, Anne mused, smiling wryly at the quaint phrase. Her smile disappeared as she remembered that they would still be working closely together until the Marini contracts were signed. So she could still expect Justin to be in touch very shortly, if not this morning.

Anne's reflections were interrupted by the telephone.

"*Buongiorno*, Signorina Hopkins," came the desk clerk's deferential tenor. "I hope you have slept well? There is a gentleman here who wishes to know if he may come up to your suite. A Signor Bradley."

Justin was here in the hotel! Anne's heart hammered wildly. "Tell him to allow me about twenty minutes to finish my—ah, toilette," she said, unwilling to reveal to either the hotel employee nor Justin himself that she wasn't even dressed yet.

"Very good, Signorina Hopkins."

Anne showered and put on a smart ivory linen pantsuit and high-heeled sandals of almost the same color. She was just giving the finishing touches to her makeup when she heard Justin's knock. She was glad he couldn't see her hand shake as she unlocked the door and opened it.

"Anne! It's a beautiful day and you look gorgeous." Before she could respond, he brought a large bouquet of exquisite anemones from behind his back and presented them to her with a courtly half bow.

Anne was moved by his thoughtfulness, and couldn't help laughing at his dramatics. "Why, Justin, they're beautiful," she breathed, accepting the flowers. As his fingers grazed hers, an electric thrill traveled up her spine, and she turned away quickly. "I'll have to find something to put these in," she explained, gesturing vaguely, feeling distracted.

"Later," he said huskily, entering the room and putting his arms lightly around her waist. She held the flowers stiffly before her, almost as a talisman to keep him at arm's length. But with an impulsive gesture he took the bouquet and tossed it onto a nearby sofa. Then he drew her close, encircling her waist with his powerful arms.

Pressed against his chest, dizzy with his heady, masculine scent, Anne yielded to his embrace, yielded to the soft lips that came down on hers with swift expertise. Gentle yet demanding, his tongue nuzzled her lips apart and she surrendered to the sweetness of the long, passionate kiss. His warm, searching tongue set an ache throbbing deep within her.

He slid one hand to her hip and drew her more tightly against his long length. Instinctively she strained even closer, letting the delicious sensation of his manly hardness pressing into her womanly softness wash over her and fill her with a warm, intense glow. His other hand crept upward and brushed her shimmering hair over one shoulder as he stroked the soft, sensitive skin of her neck with a deft, tantalizing caress. His burning lips returned to her face for a series of gentle, loving kisses on her forehead, cheeks, and lips. And then his tongue probed deeply inside her mouth once more, and a flame of desire ran through her veins as she succumbed to another urgent, hungry kiss.

When he finally broke away, Anne was overwhelmed with a realization of what she'd done. They were business associates, yet she'd returned his kisses with a wantonness she'd never exhibited even in her most intimate moments with Chuck... or with any other man. Only their first full day in Rome, and she'd been ready to submit to Justin like a sex-starved college girl!

With as much coldness in her voice as she could muster, she demanded, "Just what is your game, Justin?"

"Game?" he said reproachfully, moving away from her though his eyes were hooded with desire. He ran a hand through his hair in a frustrated gesture. "I'm not playing games with you, Anne. I've wanted to do that ever since I first saw you in Marie's office. And if you're honest with yourself, you'll admit you wanted it too."

Anne felt at a distinct disadvantage. "All right, you're an adept kisser," she acknowledged reluctantly, her lips still tingling from the scalding pressure of his mouth. "But so what? That doesn't mean I'm panting for more."

"Aren't you?" he asked with a confident grin.

Really, the man was too much! She ignored the dig and parried with a thrust of her own. "Couldn't Monica Arletti satisfy you last night? Or was she merely an appetizer?"

He seemed to take no offense.

"Temper, temper," he replied, his grin broadening.

Damn his dimples, Anne thought darkly, realizing she'd weakened her position still further by being the first to refer to last night's encounter.

But Justin was now in the best of moods. "I think we each have some explaining to do," he said indulgently, "so let's sit down and clarify matters over breakfast. I've ordered cappuccino and some food, and room service should be sending them up any time now. There will be a vase for the anemones, too."

At that very moment a knock sounded at the door. "Perfect timing," Justin said with a wink, turning to open it. A waiter glided in with a tray of *panini,* the hard, crusty rolls on which Italians breakfasted, an assortment of jams and butter, two fresh oranges, two steaming cups of cappuccino, and a terra-cotta vase.

"This way." Justin ushered the man toward the oval white table in the outer room of Anne's suite. *"Grazie, signor, grazie."*

With an unctuous *"Prego"* the man deposited the tray and was gone. The aroma of coffee, steamed milk, and cinnamon wafting from the cappuccini made Anne realize how hungry she was, and she joined Justin at the table, deciding she would be more in control of the situation once she had eaten.

Justin had arranged the anemones in the vase and was cutting the oranges into sections with a sharp knife. He offered her a segment of the juicy fruit. Anne accepted it and waited for him to resume speaking.

"I was rude last night and I have no excuse," he began with disarming frankness. "When I saw that dandified clown kissing your hand, I just saw red and I wanted to make you both uncomfortable. Petty, I'll admit. But how the hell could you let him fawn over you that way, Anne? Don't you know you're supposed to be keeping the upper hand while these delicate negotiations are going on?"

She felt herself go white and hardly knew how to answer. "I don't know what you're talking about," she said finally, stirring the foam of her cappuccino with a silver spoon. "Mario never kissed my hand. You must have misinterpreted the situation when he was examining my nail polish. He was interested in the countess's color sense."

"Nail polish! Color sense!" Justin hooted, genuinely amused. "Oh, that's a good one."

Was he jealous or was he only suggesting that she might blunder and complicate his precious negotiations with Maestro Olivetti? Anne wished she knew as she reached for a roll and broke it deliberately in two. If only the glorious flowers he'd brought weren't on the table before her, eloquently pleading his case.

"I really don't understand you, Justin," she forced herself to say in dulcet tones. "I would expect you, of all people, to know the little niceties that accompany a first meeting between potential business colleagues." She slathered half the roll with a curlicue of sweet butter and a dollop of strawberry jam. "No, I really don't understand you. If you're so concerned about what you term 'delicate negotiations,' why on earth would you jeopardize them yourself by dating the former fiancée of a man we're trying to keep happy and cooperative? Not that it's any concern of mine whom you have dinner with," she added quickly.

Justin took a long drink of his cappuccino before replying. "I don't know if Marini is deliberately misleading you, or if you're merely drawing your own inaccurate conclusions," he began acidly, "but you couldn't be more wrong. First of all, I had hoped to spend last night with you, but you went ahead and made other plans."

So he was going to try to put her in the wrong. Well, she wouldn't let him wriggle out of it so easily. Reaching calmly for another orange section, Anne looked at him levelly. "It was my understanding that you were tied up in an all-day—and perhaps all-night—session with Maestro Olivetti. I don't see that I need make any apologies whatsoever for accepting Mario's invitation."

"But I need to make apologies for dining with Monica?"

he tossed off lightly. "Her family and mine are old, old friends, Anne. I've known her since she was a kid in pigtails. You've implied that I've made a wedge between her and Mario, but that's hardly the case. I'm not responsible if her parents won't accept him as a son-in-law, and she's too cowed by them to follow her own heart."

"True," Anne conceded. Mario had explained that Monica's family didn't approve of him, would prefer she married a man with a college education and social standing in New York rather than a self-made Italian designer. "Nevertheless, I wonder that you never mentioned being so well acquainted with Marini's top model during our discussions in the countess's office, or the fact that you had resumed your old friendship with her just before our meeting."

"Our parents arranged the get-together in New York," Justin told her. "We didn't have much to say to each other except to chat about mutual acquaintances. I knew she worked for Marini, and I thought that might prove useful to us, but I didn't know then that she was his top model.

"Or"—he looked at Anne steadily—"that she was romantically involved with him. But when I discovered that you were unavailable last night, it occurred to me to do Monica the courtesy of looking her up. I also thought she might be in a position to tell me something about Marini's fall collection—the success of which, as you know, is crucial to our own business here. Over drinks at my hotel she told me about their broken engagement."

"Justin, you take the cake!" Anne pushed away her plate and glared at him. "Leaving aside your Machiavellian plan of spying on Mario through one of his models, do you really expect me to believe your only other motive was to do your duty by both your families? You talk about Monica as if she were some kind of homely misfit!"

"You don't understand," Justin retorted. "She loves Marini, although frankly I don't see what either one of you finds so irresistible about him. But Monica would never do anything that might incur her family's disapproval. She only suggested to Mario that they postpone their engagement until she could win her parents over. He flew into a rage and told her now or never. How do you think she felt when she saw him with you last night, Anne? She didn't know who you were until I told her. Sure, I played along with her, trying to make him jealous.

"You may find this hard to believe, Anne," Justin continued, "but Monica's a very insecure kid. With her looks, she was spotted by a modeling agency when she was still a teenager. She defied her parents to the extent of going into modeling full time rather than attending a good college where she might have met the right man, which is what they wanted for her. Now she's twenty-five and she's all wrapped up in the fashion world, and I suppose she'd have to marry someone like Mario because she has little conversation that would interest a man from another sphere.

"I don't see anything Machiavellian about letting her go on and on about what a genius he is at making women beautiful. She only confirms your report, which makes me feel less uneasy about the big percentage of the action Olivetti wants on behalf of his client. I'm trying to do the best on behalf of my own client, too, you know."

He certainly had a way with words, Anne thought. Or maybe it was the intensity with which he looked at her from those luminous brown eyes, which gave the ring of sincerity to his speech. Yet a part of her still didn't trust him.

"So where does all this leave us?" she asked finally.

"Friends again, I hope," he said with a dazzling smile, but Anne noted how he said the word *friends* to imply ever so much more.

"Well, it certainly wouldn't do for us to be enemies,"

she admitted reluctantly. "And we do have a working relationship to get on with. Mario invited me over to the salon today for a fitting and the grand tour. What are your plans for the afternoon?"

"Actually, I'd like to see the salon myself. Mario was present for the introductions at Maestro Olivetti's yesterday, and suggested that I ought to have a look at his operation in the near future. What do you say we go over together? Olivetti's tied up with other affairs today anyway."

"Sounds good to me," Anne said neutrally.

"Does dinner together this evening also sound good?" Justin asked with a flirtatious quirk of an eyebrow. "I'm supposed to be taking care of you for the countess, you know."

"You're too kind," she murmured with a touch of coquetry. It was hard not to fall in with Justin's banter. "It might be a good idea to compare notes while our impressions are still fresh."

"Good, that's settled," he returned pleasantly. "And now to Casa Marini."

- 5 -

ANNE AND JUSTIN emerged from the Hotel Raphael into a glorious mid-April Roman day. The cloudless, soft blue sky formed a dome over a warren of alleys lined with earth-toned buildings. Slipping his arm lightly around her waist, Justin guided her through one of the narrow passageways into the splendor of the Piazza Navona.

Anne gasped with pleasure. The square, actually an oval, was a baroque gem. There were no skyscrapers here to mar the ancient grandeur, and the squalling Roman traffic had been banned from the precincts.

"If you close your eyes you can almost hear the thunder of the great chariot races that were once held here," Justin murmured close to her ear. Anne knew he was referring to the fact that the piazza had been constructed on the ruins of the Stadium of Domitian.

She made the experiment, but instead of horses' hooves she heard the pounding of her own heart as Justin's fingertips raced seductively over her back, sending a delicious shiver up her spine. She opened her eyes quickly and her gaze flitted in turn to each of the landmarks to which Justin called her attention—the twin-towered Church of Sant'Agnese, the neighboring Palazzo Pamphili, and the triad of fountains in the center of which was Bernini's "Fountain of the Four Rivers," with its erect obelisk and white stone personifications of the Nile, the Ganges, the Danube, and the Río de la Plata.

"You've never been to Rome before?" Justin inquired as they crossed the square to the Corso Rinascimento.

Anne shook her head. "I gather you know the city well."

"Business brings me here from time to time," he acknowledged. "But with you at my side it takes on a new aura."

It wasn't so much the words as the intimate tone of his resonant voice that set Anne's heart aflutter. She tried to dismiss the compliment carelessly. "Flowers, flattery," she said lightly. "My goodness, what next, Justin?"

"I know what's next in my scenario," he said suggestively.

The invitation was unmistakable, and Anne hastily changed the subject. "Isn't that a taxi pulling into the stand up ahead, Justin?" she asked, pointing down the avenue.

"Are you so eager to go to Casa Marini?" he asked with a slight edge to his voice, but he obligingly hailed the cab.

They rode through streets lined with newly leafing trees, luxurious hotels, and elegant cafés and restaurants. Not to mention the shops! The displays of haute couture, expensive jewelry, and the leather goods for which Italy was justly famous easily rivaled Fifth and Madison Avenues for both quality and sheer quantity.

Mario's studio and salon were located on the fashionable Via Condotti. The building, faced in the ubiquitous terra-cotta stucco that seemed a Roman trademark, was distinguished by an ancient marble pillar that looked as if it had once supported a temple honoring one of the ancient Roman gods. The pillar was impacted into the stucco, and the gleaming plate glass fronting the building's street floor protected it from the elements. Behind the glass a mannequin wore a deceptively simple sun dress, with panels of canary-yellow silk alternating with a crisp white corded dimity. This novel combination of fabrics marked the dress as a Marini, as did its stark, elegant cut.

"On you it would be very nice," Justin commented, "but then, so would a gunnysack, or a barrel . . . or nothing at all." It was the first time he had spoken to her since his suggestive remark before they got into the cab, and she noted that his thoughts seemed to have remained in their single-minded groove.

"You know, Justin, I think the Roman air is affecting you," she declared, still focusing on the window of Casa Marini.

He laughed. "I doubt it's the air," he said with characteristic innuendo. And then more conversationally, "Actually the Roman air used to be notoriously unhealthy. As you probably remember from Henry James's tale of Daisy Miller."

"She caught malaria while roaming around the Colosseum at night," Anne recalled. "Although personally I've always thought she really died of a broken heart." The thought of innocent American girls getting their hearts broken in Rome caused a hollow feeling in her stomach, and she quickly suggested that they proceed to the salon.

Justin opened the brassbound plate-glass door and held it for her. Acknowledging his courtesy with a slight nod, Anne passed through the entryway into a magnificent open space with Venetian-blue glass walls dotted with cut-crystal fans that shaded the wall lights. This was the salon, the showroom of Casa Marini. Behind discreet glass cases Anne saw a selective yet spectacular array of Marini designs. Displays featuring square and oblong silk scarves patterned in unique designs of the startling hues for which Marini was celebrated and with the designer's name scrawled elegantly across one corner gave way to arrangements of mannequins garbed in Mario's latest creations for morning, afternoon, and evening wear.

"You're like Alice in Wonderland," Justin teased as he followed her from case to case, seemingly unmoved by the fantasia of fabric and color surrounding them.

"Wonderland's the word for it," Anne breathed, but she wasn't so carried away that she was oblivious of Justin's fingers gliding inside the jacket of her linen suit and resting firmly on the thin rayon blouse she wore under it. She hoped he couldn't feel the goose bumps that his touch aroused beneath the skimpy fabric.

"May I help you?" a *vendeuse* asked in gracious Italian. Justin replied in the same language that they would like to see Signor Marini. Before the saleswoman could protest that her employer was very busy, Mario himself materialized amid the languid shoppers and bustling employees.

With a deferential apology his underling left the designer and the American couple to themselves.

"I'm delighted to see you," Mario said, shaking Justin's hand and raising Anne's to his lips with Continental courtesy. "You must forgive Signora Callegari," he went on, apparently alluding to the protective saleswoman. "It is true that with only ten days before the unveiling of the spring collection, I am *molto occupato*. But I have been at the salon since five this morning, and I think I can allow some time to show you Casa Marini." Clearly Mario was proud of his elegant domain.

Mario took Anne's hand and Justin was forced—reluctantly, Anne sensed—to release his own hold on her waist. He trailed a bit behind her and Mario, and was silent as Anne oohed and ahed over the beach ensembles and resort wear. But he showed considerable enthusiasm as they reached the displays of nightgowns and lingerie toward the back of the salon.

"Now, that," he said, indicating a filmy jade-green

negligee with slightly darker satin trim, "is my idea of chic."

"There's not much to it," Anne said dryly, noting the slit sides and plunging décolletage of the diaphanous creation.

"Exactly," Justin said with a sly chuckle, and a look of understanding seemed to pass between him and Mario.

"The fitting rooms are behind that door," Mario said, indicating a large silver door at the end of the salon, just behind the display of intimate apparel. He beckoned them through it into a wide hallway off which were numerous smaller silver doors. He knocked at one, and when there was no response, led them into what seemed to Anne an unusually spacious dressing room, complete with a three-way mirror and two comfortable chairs.

"Sometimes the clients bring a guest, or a mother accompanies her daughter," Mario explained.

From the hallway they heard a woman's voice boom, "Signor Marini!" The call appeared to be taken up by the occupants of all the fitting rooms in use along the broad passageway. Now that the master's presence was known, a chorus of female voices beseeched his aid.

Anne didn't wonder that Mario's genius was in such demand. His magic seemed capable of transforming even the most unprepossessing woman into an object of envy or desire. He could make a figure look thinner here or fuller there, longer or shorter in the waist, narrower or more voluptuous at the hips. He could rivet the attention on a swanlike neck or well-shaped wrist while calling it away from less attractive parts of the body. He could make maturity alluring, and for the younger clients who were his special darlings, he could heighten their bloom and make them trend setters whose taste and chic were the talk of their set. So the siren calls came.

"You must excuse me for a moment," he told Anne and Justin apologetically. "Why don't you wait for me back in the salon, and then I'll escort you upstairs to the workrooms when I can make my escape."

Justin's hand once again found its proprietary niche at Anne's waist as he led her back to the lingerie cases. Stopping before the jade-colored nightgown he had admired earlier, he gestured toward it with his free hand and asked, "Does the countess's expense account include this sort of thing?"

"Hardly!" Anne laughed. "The Dragu purse strings open only when the purchase is on public display. You should see the lab where the famous products are brewed. Since no one ever enters it except the countess and her staff, not even the basic amenities have been provided. I'll swear it was modeled after a medieval dungeon."

"I've overheard Bessie making cracks to that effect," Justin admitted, joining in her laughter. "Still, it's a pity about the nightgown. Although, come to think of it," he added, his voice dropping an octave, "I'd rather see you with nothing on at all."

Anne shot Justin a disapproving look and began to wonder if their cappuccini had been laced with an aphrodisiac. He was certainly coming on stronger than ever today. Nevertheless, she couldn't help smiling when he chuckled in response to her flustered expression.

Anne was saved from replying by Mario's reappearance. "I am so sorry to keep you," he said, "but back there it is all 'Mario, Mario, Mario.'"

"Like the first act of *Tosca*," Justin suggested urbanely.

"Exactly. You like our Italian opera, then?" Mario addressed Justin with new respect.

"Very much," he said, "and it's also part of my bread and butter. Before coming to Rome, I was negotiating with the management of La Scala on behalf of La Tiziana."

"Ah, La Tiziana," Mario said knowledgeably. "A beautiful woman, and what a voice! *Davvero, una prima donna assoluta!*"

"In more ways than one," Justin said ruefully. "She has a prima donna's temper as well."

"The fabled redheaded temperament," Mario agreed. "But I understand she yields to masculine persuasion."

"I persuaded her to sign the contract," Justin said cryptically.

Anne didn't like all this talk of persuading redheads. "Mario, weren't we supposed to see the workrooms next?" she reminded him gently.

"*Certo*! Forgive me. Come, it is this way." He led them to a tiny wrought-iron caged elevator on the far wall. "Only two at a time, I'm afraid," he apologized. "Signor Bradley, you will follow us?"

Justin assented, though none too enthusiastically, and Anne and Mario wedged themselves into the tiny cage. As they rode to the upper floor, Mario flashed her a winning smile. "I want to thank you again for last night," he said. "You certainly know how to make business a pleasure."

"The pleasure was all mine," she answered graciously.

As they emerged from the elevator and sent the cage back down to Justin, Mario spoke again. "Anne," he began hesitantly, "about last night."

"Yes?" she encouraged him.

"Well, it's just . . . but you have intelligence. I'm sure you will guess what I have to say. I fear when I saw the woman I had hoped to marry with another man, I was overcome with jealousy and desired to make her feel a similar pain. I hope you did not think I was merely using you, or that I staged our little encounter at the restaurant. I had no idea Monica and your Mr. Bradley were going to be there, I assure you."

"You can put your mind at ease," Anne told him. "I may have noticed that you showed a certain opportune interest in the countess's nail polish," she added with a grin, "but I wasn't offended in the least."

"You are all understanding." He smiled at her with

relief. "Now I see that it was foolish to imagine there was anything between Monica and—" He broke off abruptly as the elevator arrived bearing Justin.

As Mario showed them around the workroom, Anne saw that this was obviously the heart of his enterprise. The whine of sewing machines, the purposeful scurrying of workers bearing paper patterns, bolts of fabric, and sketches, contributed to an atmosphere of productive activity.

"Would it be possible for us to see some of the clothes that will actually be included in the fall collection?" Justin asked casually.

Mario shrugged. "I can have Sandra, my best sample maker, show you one or two. But to tell you the truth, I have not yet made a final selection. I have samples made of about eighty sketches, but only fifty will be chosen for the collection, and of those maybe forty-five will eventually be cut and shipped."

The two models that Sandra showed them were characteristic Marini, a stunning leopard-printed chiffon dinner gown with leg-o'-mutton sleeves and a long slit up the left side, and a provocative pantsuit combining red denim and cobalt-blue silk taffeta. Gesturing toward the latter outfit, Mario remarked, "Other designers have started to follow me in pairing materials, but I am still way ahead of them all. Who but Marini can mix denim and taffeta, khaki and satin, lace and wool? I am also experimenting with medleys of five and six fabrics at a time. Of course, I tell you this in strict confidence," he said quickly.

"Of course," Anne echoed.

Justin met Mario's look with a grin. "Your secrets are safe with me, Signor Marini," he assured the designer. "Not only is it in the countess's interest that your fall collection be kept a secret until the official unveiling, but I wouldn't have the vocabulary to describe your fashions if I wanted to. Anne's the expert in that department."

"*Sì, sì,* just as I thought," Mario said. "I do not share the paranoia that is common to this industry. Some say I am too trusting, but perhaps I am merely too vain to believe that my designs could be duplicated even if there should be leaks. Of course, spies and stolen sketches are quite another matter. I have plainclothes guards watching the elevator downstairs at all times for two weeks before the show, and no one comes up here to the workroom except authorized personnel."

When the tour of the workroom was completed, Mario ushered Anne and Justin into his adjoining studio. The studio was a large, well-lit room whose only furniture was a long worktable littered with sketches, doodles, stray samples of material, and a low round stool.

"Here is where I design my collections," Mario explained. "The shows actually begin with the selection of fabrics, which I do in October at the Pescio factory in Como. The fabrics are my inspiration, though I work from sketches rather than draping. Me, I do not need to drape. In my head I can see exactly what each type of material will do—how it will hang, where it will cling, what design will bring out its particular qualities. I am like the composer who can hear the symphony in his head before he transcribes a single note of the score."

Their final visit was to the business office on the third floor of Casa Marini. Once again Anne and Mario ascended together in the minuscule elevator and Justin followed by himself. The marketing and order departments were much less hectic than the chaotic workroom, and apparently equally productive. Anne found Signor Martinelli, the marketing manager, as pleasant as he was shrewd, and the two of them soon became engrossed in comparing notes about marketing techniques in their respective industries.

Justin listened attentively to their conversation, as if monitoring it to judge whether she really knew what she was doing, Anne thought with a shade of annoyance.

Mario, however, shifted from foot to foot as if bored by all this shop talk outside his area of expertise. Finally he said, "Paolo, I can see you and Anne have much to discuss. Perhaps you can make an appointment for tomorrow. You see, she is scheduled for a fitting this afternoon, and I am sure she and Signor Bradley would like to take some time to eat beforehand."

"Forgive me," Signor Martinelli said hastily. "What do you say, Anne—I may call you that, yes? And you will call me Paolo. We will continue our conversation over lunch tomorrow. That is convenient, yes?"

"That sounds lovely, Paolo. I'll look forward to it," Anne replied. She thought she saw Justin repress a grimace and felt an inward smile. With his sensitive face and blond Northern Italian coloring, Paolo Martinelli was something of an Italian Paul Newman. She wasn't about to reassure Justin that men in their forties didn't interest her. Let him feel as uncomfortable about Paolo's gallantry as she'd felt about Linda Beth's coquetry.

Mario's next words were to make Justin actually glower. "You know, Signor Bradley," the designer said thoughtfully as they waited for the elevator, "I think it might be just as well if Anne and I lunched together just the two of us today. You see, we will have a lot to discuss about the wardrobe I have promised the countess to provide for her, and I do not think you would find these details terribly interesting."

"Oh, I don't know about that," Justin countered a trifle belligerently. "You see, Signor Marini, I find everything about Anne Hopkins interesting. *Very* interesting."

"Indeed? I think I can understand that," Mario said smoothly. Far from looking offended, he seemed to brighten at Justin's remark. Perhaps he thought that if Justin was interested in her he'd leave Monica alone, Anne conjectured.

She felt both men were waiting for her to speak. If

she and Mario were going to discuss her wardrobe, she actually preferred that Justin not be present. For one thing, she wanted to talk to Mario about the dress she would need for their date that evening. For another, if Mario was going to criticize her taste, as he had the previous evening, she would be less embarrassed if he did so without Justin hearing.

She smiled sweetly at Justin and said, "Many thanks for the compliment, but I think Mario has a point. And it would give you a few hours for rest, which I suspect you haven't had much of lately between your commitments in Milan and those here in Rome."

"My turn for a little beauty sleep, eh?" he asked facetiously. "All right, then, I'll leave you to your discussions. I'll meet you in the lobby of the Raphael at eight sharp, Anne."

From the way he said it, she wasn't sure if it was a threat or an invitation.

- 6 -

ANNE LUNCHED WITH Mario at a charming trattoria on Via Frattini on fettuccine *all'uovo*, broad egg noodles in a rich butter and cheese sauce.

"You can afford to sample our Roman pasta," Mario commented with an appreciative scrutiny of her slender figure. "In fact, you are so like a model it will not be difficult to alter the outfits I have in mind for you. Perhaps we must take up the hemlines a few centimeters, and let out some material in the bust, but that is all."

"And what are these outfits you have in mind for me?" Anne asked gaily as they clinked glasses of the light white wine that Mario had informed her had the picturesque name of Est Est Est.

"Trust me, Annina—you do not object to an Italian nickname, I hope?" he said amiably. "In a few days you will have a complete Marini wardrobe hanging in your closet, and I guarantee you will approve."

She told him she needed a dress for that evening. She didn't tell him that her date was with Justin, but he apparently remembered the attorney's final words in the salon.

"Ah, yes, you are dining tonight with your handsome

colleague, Signor Bradley," he said, his black eyes sparkling. "And perhaps he is something more than a colleague as well, yes?"

Anne looked into her wineglass. "I hardly know him," she murmured. "We only met just before this trip to Italy."

Mario shrugged. *"Che importa?"* he asked rhetorically. "Me, I believe in the love at first sight. When Monica came to my salon looking for a job, I said to myself at once, 'Here is the woman I will marry.'" A shadow of pain crossed his face. "But never mind that, we were talking about you and Signor Bradley. He cares for you, Annina, that is evident."

"He cares for every attractive woman," Anne found herself saying. "I was warned about him by friends in New York."

Mario shook his head emphatically. "You should not listen to what people say," he scolded her. "Your Justin Bradley may have played the Romeo many times, yet I feel he has more than a passing interest in you. And if the feeling is mutual, I tell you frankly, Annina, it is *pazzìa*—madness—to let suspicion stand in the way of true love."

Anne gave a light laugh. "I don't know about true love, Mario."

"I do," the designer said authoritatively. "And I tell you again, do not let gossip make up your mind for you. Give Signor Bradley a chance, Annina. Do not close the door before it is even open."

After lunch Anne and Mario strolled back to the salon in leisurely fashion as Mario pointed out various landmarks along the Via Frattini. Anne bought some colorful postcards of Rome from a street vendor to send to her parents and friends.

When they returned to Casa Marini, Mario selected a dress for her to wear that evening—a dream of shimmering aquamarine watered silk with a snug bodice supported by the thinnest spaghetti straps.

"You see?" he said triumphantly as she emerged from the dressing room to model the gown for him. "Only a tuck here and there and it will be a perfect fit. But something is lacking . . . *aspetta*."

He scurried off, returning a few minutes later with a velvet box. "This necklace is on loan to Casa Marini for the showing of my collection," he explained as he fastened the pendant of fire opals scattered in a fretwork of eighteen-karat gold around her throat. "A perfect complement to my dress!" he proclaimed.

"Oh, Mario, I couldn't," Anne protested, seeing the initials of one of Italy's most illustrious jewelers on the box.

"Do not worry." Mario dismissed her fears. "You can return the necklace tomorrow. This dress simply cries out for it. I am sure Signor Bradley will keep the Roman *ladri* at bay for the evening, and you can put the necklace in the hotel safe overnight if that will make you feel more comfortable."

"It is lovely," Anne acquiesced, gazing at her reflection in the pier glass in the corridor outside the dressing room. The fire opals glimmered back at her, lending new lustre to her blue eyes, which were only a shade lighter than the aquamarine dress.

"Signor Bradley will be enthralled," Mario said softly.

Mario's words came back to Anne as she greeted Justin just before eight in front of the antique sleigh that graced the lobby of the Hotel Raphael.

"You're a vision," he breathed as his eyes caressed her in a way that made her heart leap to her throat. He brought his lips to hers for a chaste kiss. Even that brief contact made Anne dizzy with longing.

"I guess Marini knows what he's about after all," Justin remarked as they left the hotel together. "Frankly, his own clothes are a little too campy for my taste, and

I wasn't sure I was going to like you so much as Marie's 'Marini girl,'" he confessed.

Anne barely heard the words, so conscious was she of being alone with Justin in the most romantic of cities, and of his warm fingers clasped over her bare shoulder as they turned onto the Corso Vittorio Emanuele.

"You look good yourself," she managed brightly, taking in the chocolate-brown suit, maize-colored shirt, and burnt sienna tie that harmonized so well with his warm coloring. "By the way, where are we off to?" She hardly cared; Justin's magnetic presence eclipsed the scenery and evoked a potent yearning in her.

"Somewhere special," he assured her in a low voice. "We have a reservation at a *ristorante* on the Vìcolo delle Bollete, which is close to the Fountain of Trevi. I thought it was auspiciously named—La Fòrza del Destino."

"The force of destiny," Anne translated. "Named after the Verdi opera, no doubt." She didn't know about destiny; she felt overwhelmed by the force drawing her to Justin.

"Are you up for walking?" Justin asked. "It's not too far to the restaurant, and I thought we might stop a moment at the Trevi Fountain and throw in some coins. That ensures a return visit to Rome, you know."

"All right," Anne said dreamily, drinking in the balmy night air and gazing at the radiant white marble of the Victor Emmanuel Monument, which glowed like a lighted birthday cake in the distance.

She was so fascinated by the myriad sights, sounds, and smells that she hardly noticed when they reached the small piazza where the famed Trevi Fountain was situated. The rushing of the waters above the hubbub of Roman street life drew her attention.

"Prepare for the descent," Justin told her, running his fingertips lightly down her bare arm until he found her hand and grasped it tightly. Together they joined the throngs hurrying down the stone staircase to the enormous baroque extravaganza of stonework and statuary presided over by a fierce Neptune astride fiery marble steeds and surrounded by youthful Tritons. The wall behind was a palatial façade dotted with bas-reliefs of allegorical figures, grottoes, niches, and massive heaps of broken rock. A semicircular cascade of water exploded from a central precipice, while smaller jets gushed, spouted, and splashed from other crevices in the stone, and from the open mouths and nostrils of myriad phantasmagoric sea monsters. Taking it all in, Anne was nevertheless acutely aware of Justin's strong fingers entwined with hers.

They watched as coins of many nations flew through the air to join the glittering array of metal in the pool. When Justin released her hand to dig in his pocket for some lire, Anne felt an unexpected sense of abandonment.

"There's a special ritual," he said, placing a coin in her right hand and gently revolving her so she stood with her back toward the fountain. She turned mechanically, conscious only of the erotic sensation of Justin's fingertips on her bare flesh, of the sweet warmth of his breath in her ear as he spoke.

"Toss the coin over your right shoulder," he instructed her, "and the genie of the fountain will grant your wish to revisit Rome."

They threw their coins simultaneously, turning quickly to see them land amid the others. Anne's shoulder grazed the nubby texture of Justin's suit jacket, and a current of electric desire flowed through her.

They looked into each other's eyes, and Anne knew her own gaze mirrored Justin's look of barely contained passion. "Actually the street urchins clean out the place in the wee hours," he told her huskily, "but I can't resist all the same." His voice dipped a register as he went on, "And there's something else I can't resist."

With a will of its own, her body melted into his as

he drew her against him. Amid the deafening roar of the waters his face bent toward hers, and his tongue circled her lips, then parted them. Anne returned his fierce kiss with an urgency that stunned her. It felt so right to be pressing against his angular length, to be yielding her mouth to his demanding lips. Time stood still as his arms closed over her back and his fingers caressed the sensitive skin beneath the French braid of her hair. Anne had never felt so totally possessed by a man before, and she found herself wanting to prolong the moment to eternity.

"*La fòrza del destino,*" Justin murmured when at last he took his lips from hers and gazed intently into her eyes.

She could hear her own breathing as she met his languorous gaze. How she longed to return to the oblivion of sensuality into which he had drawn her. In Justin's embrace she had experienced a feeling of homecoming, as if nothing were more natural than to be held in his powerful arms, to allow his authoritative lips to draw the nectar from her answering kiss.

"*La fòrza del destino,*" she repeated, trying to recapture her dignity. "Isn't that where we're eating tonight?" She averted her eyes from his penetrating look in confusion. "I am beginning to feel ravenous."

"For food?" he teased, his voice hoarse with need.

They looked at each other, their eyes speaking volumes amid the floodlights of the fountain.

"I'd like to go to the restaurant now," Anne said, knowing that what she really wanted was to yield to him completely.

"Then we'll do just that," Justin said lightly, though disappointment shone in his eyes. His hand found the small of her back, and he escorted her up the staircase to the piazza.

The restaurant, with its gold brocade walls, old marble fireplace, frosted-glass chandeliers, and mirrored wall sconces, exuded an atmosphere that was both cozy and elegant. Delicious aromas seemed to waft from every table.

"Signor Bradley! It is truly a pleasure to see you again," the maître d' greeted Justin effusively.

"The pleasure is mine, Alberto," Justin replied in flawless Italian. "As you can see, I have brought a friend, Miss Anne Hopkins, to sample your delicious pasta with me this evening."

"How do you do, Miss Hopkins?" Alberto replied in careful English. "I am delighted to meet a friend of Signor Bradley's. He is the guardian angel of our family."

At Anne's startled look the maître d' continued, "Through Signor Bradley's good offices two of my daughters have won full scholarships to the conservatory—Carla to study voice and Mana the piano."

"Please, Alberto," Justin protested hastily. "I had nothing to do with Maria's success, and I only said a word about Carla to a friend."

"Ah, but the friend just happened to be La Tiziana, the famous diva!" Alberto reminded him. He explained to Anne, "The first time Signor Bradley came here, he happened to comment on the operatic name of the restaurant. Somehow we got on the subject of Carla's musical abilities. I told him how she longed to make a career of opera, but that with four other daughters to support, I could not afford the many years of training." He spread his hands in a helpless gesture.

"As luck would have it," Alberto went on, "that season La Tiziana was singing at the Rome Opera. Your friend Mr. Bradley set up an audition with her for my Carla. In turn, the great coloratura arranged an audition with the head of the voice department at the conservatory. It seems he had been one of her own voice teachers some years earlier at Juilliard. La Tiziana and Signor Agretti were responsible for the scholarship. But it was Signor Bradley who set everything in motion and—"

"Not at all, Alberto," Justin interrupted. "It was Carla's extraordinary voice that made everything possible."

"You are too modest," Alberto insisted. "Even with a scholarship," he told Anne, "there are additional expenses that we could hardly afford if Signor Bradley had not generously loaned us the money—"

"Nonsense, Alberto. I consider those loans among my best investments."

"You are the angel of our family, Signor Bradley," Alberto insisted. "But in my gratitude I forget you have come here to eat. I am detaining you. Marco!" he called, and a young waiter hurried over to them. "Our best table for Signor Bradley and his most beautiful friend."

Anne smiled at hearing herself described as "*bellissima*," but she was glad of the proprietary pride in Justin's eyes as he grinned back at her. They followed the waiter to an intimate table for two by a window overlooking the tiny Piazza di Trevi. No sooner were they seated than the wine steward appeared with a bottle of vintage Orvieto.

"Compliments of Signor Squatrito," he said, opening the wine and pouring some into Justin's glass.

"Alberto," Justin explained to Anne, as he sipped and nodded his approval. The wine steward then filled both their glasses and departed. "His eldest daughter really does have a magnificent voice, and Rosa is equally gifted at the keyboard. I'm sure those two could have made it to the conservatory without anyone's help, only it never occurred to the family that the girls could win full scholarships. Their only musical training came from the choirmaster at a local church, and he had neither the means nor the connections to aid them."

"Being a guardian angel is nothing to apologize for," Anne teased him, but her voice was full of appreciation for his generosity. She wondered at the pleasure it had given her to hear the maître d's favorable account of Justin. Could the passion that had overwhelmed her at the Trevi Fountain have something to do with this new eagerness to learn good things of Justin Bradley?

"It's you who are like an angel," Justin turned the compliment deftly. "The moment you walked into Marie's office, I felt as if one of the three graces from Botticelli's 'Primavera' had come to life." He lifted his wineglass in a toast, and Anne raised her own glass and clinked it against his.

"To the force of destiny—our destiny," he murmured as they brought the crystal goblets to their lips. Once again their gazes locked, and Anne looked away in confusion. He'd said it as if he really believed they could have a future together.

Just then the young waiter Marco returned to take their order. At Justin's suggestion Anne agreed to share a plate of spaghetti *alla carbonara* with him for the first course, to be followed by roast veal with new peas for Anne and a spicier veal dish for Justin.

When the pasta arrived—thin noodles cooked *al dente* and drenched in a rich egg, cheese, and bacon sauce—Anne realized how famished she was.

"This isn't just pasta, it's ambrosia," she told Justin, filling her fork again. "I suppose I ought to feel guilty," she went on, "because I promised the countess I wouldn't overindulge on Roman cuisine. But it's so delicious I can't work up the least bit of remorse for eating every bite."

"Just save some room for dessert," Justin advised, a wicked gleam in his eyes. "They have a fantastic selection of pastries and homemade ice cream here. My own favorite is the *monte bianco*—a mountain of freshly whipped cream flavored with chestnut purée and served in the lightest of meringues."

"It sounds sinful." Anne sighed, taking another sip of her Orvieto.

"It is. But why not live a little?" he coaxed. The double entendre in his voice sent pinpricks of arousal to the core of Anne's being.

Changing the subject, she asked him, "So, what did you make of Casa Marini?"

He took a sip of Orvieto and considered thoughtfully. "I don't know," he answered. "Some of the clothes seemed a bit far out to me. Like that denim and taffeta pantsuit, for instance. Did you like it?"

"I thought it was rather stylish," Anne admitted. "But you know, Justin, neither that outfit nor the leopard gown will be shown in the collection."

"What do you mean?" he asked. "Mario said—"

"He said he hadn't yet made a final selection, remember, and I'm sure he means to keep the actual collection top secret. I could tell he wasn't happy with the sleeves on the gown—he kept frowning at them—and I think he only showed us those two samples to placate our curiosity. The comment about the medley of fabrics was a genuine slip, though. He didn't mean to tell us that; I could hear it in his voice."

"You're a sharp lady," Justin said, his eyes glowing with admiration. "But now I'm even more worried. I couldn't really get many details out of Monica. Just that the collection would be fabulous, and a dozen other superlatives."

"I'm sure it will be," Anne said complacently, reaching for a breadstick. "What makes you think otherwise."

"Well, you mentioned in your report that Mario's backing comes from that Pescio fabric factory. It's obvious that his designs call a lot of attention to the fabrics, and I just wonder if he doesn't go overboard in an effort to please his financers, perhaps overlooking what the customer really wants."

"I can see how you'd make that inference, but believe me, it's totally unfounded. Mario would only accept the backing of a fabric firm he was enthusiastic about, and his creative use of materials is precisely one of the reasons the younger members of the jet set are flocking to him. If anyone can capture the young, affluent female executive market for the countess, it's Mario Marini."

"What about the Marini cosmetics line?" he asked. "Has he told you his ideas for that?"

"I broached the subject at lunch today," Anne reported. "Mario said he had some inspirations, but he wanted to read my report first, and make some doodles and notes over the weekend so we can get together early next week and discuss them."

Justin frowned. "So you have no idea what he's cooking up? It's hard for me to negotiate with Olivetti on that basis. I mean, even if he's a genius in haute couture, how do you know he can cut it in cosmetics?"

"I'm not worried," Anne said. "I'm sure Mario will come up with some innovative ideas. In the meantime I plan to discuss distribution with Paolo Martinelli tomorrow. He can tell me which stores are already carrying Marini fashions, and I can think up some promotional activities accordingly."

"Oh, yeah, that Martinelli guy," Justin said sourly. "The personification of machismo. You'd better watch out for him, Anne. I think he has more than marketing mixes on his mind."

"I see you picked up some jargon this afternoon," she said noncommittally.

"Anne, that guy has his eye on you."

"It didn't strike me as an evil eye." She laughed. "Besides, he was wearing a wedding ring."

"So what? You've never heard of cheaters? Anne, I'm serious. You're a very beautiful woman, and it's obvious these Italian men appreciate that. It could really blow our whole deal apart if you naïvely let yourself be charmed into what could become a very sticky situation."

So he wasn't jealous of Paolo; he only feared for his delicate negotiations! Anne struggled to control her rising anger. "You forget, Justin, that I am surrounded by males in the marketing division of Dragu Cosmetics. Not to mention that many of the department store personnel I do business with are also men. So you can stop treating me as if I were Little Red Riding Hood making her first journey into a forest peopled with big bad wolves."

Justin toyed with his wineglass for a long moment before answering. "I'm sorry if I implied that you were a babe in the woods," he apologized finally. "But Italy is not America, and that's especially true when it comes to attitudes toward women. There are far fewer women executives in Rome than in New York, you know, and I doubt that your Paolo is used to professional relationships with women. Marini either, for that matter. I'm only cautioning you to watch your step."

"I hear you, Justin. I heard you the first time," Anne said stiffly.

"Oh, Anne!" He reached across the table and captured both her hands. "I can see I've put my foot in my mouth, but let's not quarrel. I promise, not another word about Italian stallions. Okay?"

"Okay," she relented, thawing under his beseeching gaze.

Marco brought their main courses and for a few moments they ate in silence. When Anne resumed the conversation, it was to ask, "So what did you do with yourself this afternoon?"

"I made a few phone calls," he told her. "There was a message at my hotel from Olivetti's office, and when I talked to his secretary, she suggested I drop by in the morning to pick up a preliminary draft of an agreement based on my discussions with the maestro yesterday. I'll be spending tomorrow going over it with a fine-toothed comb. Then I called Marie in New York and chatted a bit. She wanted to know if you had hit it off with Marini, and of course I told her you two get along beautifully."

"I'm planning to check in with her tomorrow," Anne said. "I'm sure she'll be interested in a report on my lunch with Paolo and general impressions of the salon."

"She has a lot of confidence in you," Justin said. "I

think maybe she's grooming you to take over when she retires."

"She doesn't plan to retire," Anne said firmly. "Dragu is her whole life. I think it's a bit sad really, not to mention ironic. Here she is selling dreams of romance to millions of women, and she's never been married herself. I don't know if there's even been a special man in her life."

"One of the senior partners at my firm mentioned something about Marie being in love once," Justin said thoughtfully. "I wasn't paying too much attention and I don't recall the details or what happened. She must have been a very striking woman in her younger years, though a bit too commanding for my taste. Slender redheads with luminescent blue eyes are my idea of perfection," he added, with a wolfish leer.

"Very charmingly put, but perfection is hardly accurate," Anne returned, embarrassed. "Haven't you noticed that my mouth is too wide and I'm too tall?"

"I love your mouth. It reminds me of Ingrid Bergman's. Sensuous, and ever so kissable," he murmured seductively. "And you're not so tall—not over five-eight, are you?"

"Five-seven in my stocking feet. I just meant that women are supposed to be petite."

"Says who?" Justin challenged. "What about models? Speaking of which, from the gleam in Marini's eyes whenever he looks at you, I wonder if he isn't plotting to persuade you into making a career change."

"Me, model for Casa Marini? I'm sure the idea never entered his head." Nevertheless Anne felt flattered that it had entered Justin's. "In any case, I have no interest in changing careers, and even if I did, I'm a few inches too short for modeling. And if I go on eating like this"— she pushed back her empty plate—"I'll be more than a few pounds too fat for it!"

"I can't picture you fat," Justin protested.

"Oh, but you're dining with a former chubby child," she told him.

"So are you," he informed her with a conspiratorial grin.

Anne was surprised. "I don't believe it!"

"It's true, though. Banana splits were my undoing. Then, when I was about twelve, I discovered girls and decided there were sweeter things in life than sundaes."

"I was a candy-bar addict," Anne confessed. "But I gave up chocolate a few months before the tryouts for cheerleading and the aquaettes."

"And you've never cheated since," Justin teased. "Tell you what, let's celebrate our mutual willpower with that *monte bianco* I was telling you about. There's no chocolate in it, so you don't have to worry about becoming addicted all over again."

"No, just about being able to get through the door of this restaurant," Anne joked.

"We could split one," Justin urged, and in his animated face Anne glimpsed the little boy who had so relished his banana splits. "Only half the calories that way."

"True, but half of how many calories? Never mind, you've convinced me I have to try it."

They fed each other spoonfuls of the luscious concoction, laughing as they made astronomical estimates of the number of calories in every bite. Anne couldn't remember when she'd last felt so lighthearted, so relaxed.

"One billion million zillion calories," she declared, spooning the final dollop of whipped cream into Justin's waiting mouth.

"Shouldn't that be one million billion trillion zillion? Trillions come before zillions, don't they?"

"The hairsplitting logic of a lawyer," Anne said, shaking a finger at him playfully. "Anyway, I'm glad they never heard of *monte biancos* in Richmond. I'm not sure I could have given them up as easily as I did candy bars."

"Well, the candy bars don't seem to have done any harm to your complexion." His eyes traveled over her face, then rested on the necklace Mario had lent her. "That's some piece of jewelry you're wearing," he remarked. "A Christmas bonus from Marie?"

"Hardly." Anne smiled at the idea. "Her Christmas bonuses consist of a year's supply of whatever beauty products she thinks will be the most becoming to each woman employee. The men get something added to their paycheck, although the value of the cosmetics is probably greater. The necklace is a loan from Mario. One of the models is going to wear it in the show next week. I didn't want to take it," she admitted, "but Mario insisted."

Justin frowned. "It's very becoming." Then he asked, "Are you tired or would you enjoy a moonlit stroll to the Colosseum?"

"The Colosseum, definitely," she answered. "The walk will take off a few of those zillion plus calories we've just consumed."

Despite the late hour, the Colosseum was aswarm with tourists, pilgrims who had come to kiss the consecrated black cross at the center of the former stadium, young and not-so-young lovers, and what seemed to Anne's astonished eyes to be an army of cats.

"My goodness!" she exclaimed as one of the stray felines brushed past her ankle. "I had no idea that Rome was such a cat lover's paradise."

Justin chuckled. "Oh, yes. They seem to dote on the Colosseum and the Forum in particular. They're harmless, though." Despite his assurance his arm tightened protectively around her shoulder.

Gazing at the tiers of ruined, grass-grown travertine arches illuminated by both moonlight and floodlights, Anne was awed. She found Justin's protective arm strangely welcome.

"It really is impressive," she said as they continued to look at the jagged silhouette of the huge amphitheater.

"'A ruin—yet what a ruin,' was how Byron described it, I think."

"It's understandable that all the British Romantic poets gravitated to Rome, isn't it?" he commented. His fingers left her shoulder and traveled slowly upward, tracing seductive circles at the base of her throat above the necklace, and then on each cheek.

"Are you cold?" he asked as Anne began to shiver.

"A little," she said, hoping he didn't guess that her sudden tremors were caused by the magic caress of his fingers rather than the damp Roman air. "It was just that sudden breeze," she hedged as he solicitously massaged her shoulders to warm them.

"Would you like to wear my jacket?"

"Really, I'm all right now," she replied. "What were you saying about the Romantic poets?"

He continued to massage her shoulders and arms. "Just that I can understand how they fell under the spell of this city. One of these days I'll show you the house where Keats died," he said against her ear, then planted a burning kiss on the lobe. "Your skin is so soft there," he murmured.

As if mesmerized, she stood rooted to the spot as he nibbled her ear more boldly. "Justin," she began weakly, but he quickly tilted her face to his and stopped her protest with searing lips. His hands blazed a tantalizing trail down her bare back. "You feel warm now," he whispered before bringing his mouth down on hers for another passionate kiss. This time his hands cupped the soft swell of her breasts, and Anne felt her nipples strain against the gossamer fabric of her dress, as if yearning for his touch.

Justin gave a low groan and molded her against himself more tightly. Feeling the unmistakable press of his arousal against her thigh, she heard an answering groan from her own throat as her entire being turned to molten desire. Panicked by the intensity of her passion, she forced herself to pull away from his embrace.

"Justin," she said, her voice tremulous, "I think I'd better go back to my hotel. The combination of jet lag and all the good food and wine is taking its toll. Suddenly I'm very sleepy."

"We'll go back to your hotel, then," he said cryptically, and Anne wondered if he expected to accompany her to her room. Her heart raced furiously, and tiny goose bumps formed on her arms.

"You're cold again," Justin said with concern, drawing her against him. "Come on, we'll find a cab.

"Anne, my beautiful Anne," he whispered in her ear as soon as he'd given their driver directions to the Raphael. "I want to make love to you," he said fiercely as he rained soft kisses over her hair, neck, and shoulders.

Desire and apprehension warred within her. "It's been a lovely evening, Justin, but a long one," she said weakly. "I really am very tired."

Cupping her chin, he compelled her to look into his glittering eyes. "Anne, the evening's ending too soon for me. But it doesn't have to if you don't want it to. Let me stay with you tonight. Please, let me love you."

She was helpless with longing. She ached with need for him. In just a short while he had invaded the reserve she had cloaked herself in to avoid being hurt again. He had charmed her and made her laugh like a schoolgirl, and his knowing fingers and lips had awakened a passion she had too long denied was a part of her nature. Damn him, why had he hurtled her into this maelstrom of conflicting emotions? For though her every instinct cried, "Yes, Justin, make love to me tonight," her inner demon was simultaneously screaming, "No! Don't risk it. Get hold of yourself."

"Anne, say yes. I know you want me, too. Say yes, *carissima,* yes."

She knew it would be useless to repeat that she was tired, knew that Justin had felt the response of her aching flesh to his touch. Fighting the desire that raged through her, she said, "I can't treat sex so casually, Justin."

"What makes you think it will be casual?" he murmured, drawing her into his arms. "Let me show you otherwise." His lips found her earlobe and his tongue flicked over the sensitive skin.

"Justin, stop, please. I can't," she pleaded with him, wrenching away from his embrace. "I just can't." She felt as if she were being torn apart, and she took deep breaths to calm herself.

"Anne, I've never wanted a woman so much, damnit." His voice was ragged with frustration. He raked his fingers through his hair and gave a long sigh.

"Maybe it's just that no woman has ever said no to you before," she said, trying to muster up her original distrust and hostility toward him. But it was useless. "We don't always get everything we want in life, Justin," she added in a softer voice.

"I don't just want you, Anne. I need you. We could be so good for each other." He took her hand and let the warm touch of his fingertips lightly stroking her palm plead his case.

She willed her fingers to stop shaking. "I'm sorry, Justin." She felt dazed and numb.

He let her hand lie still in his as he said gently, "He hurt you pretty badly, didn't he? I promise it won't be like that with me."

She turned startled eyes on him. How had he guessed about Chuck? Or was it only a shot in the dark? "What makes you think..." she began, but he put a finger to her lips and stopped her.

"I don't think, I know. It's obvious you've been hurt very deeply. I promise you again, it will be different with me. I wouldn't hurt you for the world."

If only she could believe him. But without his meaning to, his probing of the old wound had reopened it. "I can't talk about it, Justin. Please, just let me... let me be."

"Let you be? Anne, I want to let you be the loving, passionate woman you really are. Just give me a chance, darling. Don't shut me out." Again he ran his fingers through his hair.

That was what Mario had said—to give Justin a chance. But she mustn't give him the chance to hurt her as Chuck had. She knew that this charming, compelling, cultured man had the power to cause her more pain than she'd ever experienced before. But it was such an effort to resist him!

"I need to know you better, Justin," she whispered.

"I've known you all my life," he murmured, sheltering her once again in his masterful embrace. "You're the woman of my dreams."

"Give me time," she moaned, her heart warmed by his sweet words.

He sighed against her ear. "Patience isn't my strong suit, darling."

"We can continue to see each other," Anne began feebly.

"Continue to see each other!" he exclaimed. "Of course we'll continue to see each other. I know Marie wants you to meet a lot of people over here, but don't go scheduling any business dinners. Now tell me we have a date for tomorrow night, and the night after that, and the next night, and the next," he said firmly.

Anne laughed freely and some of the tension between them eased. "You're a very persuasive man, Justin Bradley. My evenings are all yours." She was pleased that he had so readily committed all the ensuing nights to her. That must mean there were no other women—not in Rome, at least.

"Oh, *carissima,* I want more than your evenings," he said huskily. In the kiss that followed, the insistent pressure of his velvety lips, the hungry probing of his expert tongue, and the seductive stroking of his practiced fingers told her exactly what he wanted. When the cab braked to a halt outside the Hotel Raphael, she tore herself away from his arms and fled from the car. But it wasn't Justin Bradley she was running away from—it was her own turbulent emotions.

· 7 ·

BRIGHT AND EARLY the next morning, Anne stopped briefly at one of the cafés in the Piazza Navona for a cappuccino and one of the hard doughnut-shaped rolls flavored with fennel seeds that an obliging waiter told her were called *taralli*. Then she set off for the Dragu salon on the Via Nazionale near the Piazza della Republica. Since she would be talking to the countess in the afternoon, she considered it expedient to first pay a visit to the Rome salon, which the countess had more than once told Anne she should do. Having familiarized herself with the salon, she would also be able to advise the countess on the logistics of setting up a Marini boutique there after the products had been manufactured.

As the taxi maneuvered through the infamous Roman traffic jams, past houses, hotels, palaces, churches, and monuments in weathered shades of ocher, brown, gray, brick, and tan, Anne thought with pleasant anticipation about her date with Justin to spend the late afternoon sightseeing around the Piazza di Spagna and then have dinner in the bohemian section of Trastevere. She imagined his clean-cut, boyishly attractive face with its frame of tousled brown hair, and his lean, virile physique.

Remembering how he had lightly stroked her breasts, bringing the nipples to taut peaks of desire, during that final passionate kiss in the taxi the night before, she felt a thrill of yearning. It had taken all her willpower to restrain herself from telling him she'd changed her mind and inviting him to spend the night with her after all. Yet she was glad now she had resisted the impulse. Justin's ardent endearments and even more ardent advances had plunged her into a tumultuous whirlpool of sensation. But in the cold light of day she questioned his true motives. She knew all too well that a man could sound sincere without truly being so.

"*Signorina,*" the cabby broke into her reverie, "*Siamo qui.*"

"*Dove?* Oh, yes," Anne said, recognizing the brass-plated Venetian-blue door that was a trademark of Dragu salons all over the world. "*Grazie,*" she told the man, reaching into her purse for money to pay the fare.

She had phoned from the hotel and the salon's director was expecting her. Signora Gemini was a tall, imposing woman, not unlike the countess in her majestic air, though at least twenty years younger and with dark hair, olive skin, and aquiline features. She was also a good deal softer and warmer in manner than the countess, and the two women chatted easily in the director's high-ceilinged, sumptuously appointed office on the salon's fifth floor.

"We have a lovely view of the city," Signora Gemini told Anne, motioning her to a large bay window from which Anne could see a progression of red-tiled rooofs, belfries, clock towers, wooded hills, the yellow waters of the Tiber, and the gleaming dome of St. Peter's in the distance. "Have you had a chance to familiarize yourself at all with our *bella città* yet?"

"Not as much as I'd like to," Anne replied, "but I hope to see more while I'm here. The countess told you the purpose of my visit?"

The question was only a formality, for Anne had been in the countess's office on special summons during one of her supposed days of rest when the old woman had called Signora Gemini to explain their plans for the Marini line.

"Of course, of course," the dark-haired woman said graciously. "I think this collaboration with Mario Marini is a wonderful idea. Here at Dragu Roma we are also losing the younger generation to the newer establishments, but Mario Marini is the idol of the young and will bring them back to us."

Anne smiled briefly at this portrayal of Mario as a contemporary pied piper. "Do you know Signor Marini personally?" she asked.

"Alas, no, I count on you to introduce us at the proper moment. You are discussing the new line with him now, I believe?"

"We've met several times, and we'll be getting together next week to discuss colors, containers, scents, and what not," Anne explained. "But right now Mario is preoccupied with making the final selections for his showing. Next week, when the selection is complete and it's a question of merely matching accessories, rehearsing, and last-minute details, he thought he'd have more time."

"Mother of God!" Signora Gemini rolled her eyes to the pale-blue ceiling. "Merely matching accessories and so forth! My child, that's the most chaotic part! Next week Casa Marini will be a madhouse. But I am sure if he promised you, he will find the time," she added quickly.

"He told me he was going to jot down some ideas over the weekend," Anne explained. "In the meantime I'm having lunch with his marketing director this afternoon to discuss some of the distribution and promotion angles."

"Ah, yes, that is a good idea," Signora Gemini said. "You should also get together with our marketing people

during your stay. Come, I will make the introductions
and you can arrange an appointment. Then I will have
my assistant give you a tour of the salon."

When Anne emerged from the gleaming white marble
confines of Dragu Roma an hour and a half later, her
head was awhirl with Italian names. It seemed Signora
Gemini's assistant had presented her to everyone in the
building, from treatment girls to fashionable customers,
save for the executives whom the director herself had
introduced to Anne. The salon was much like the one in
New York, only on a slightly smaller scale, with rooms
for heat treatments, massage, exercise classes, manicure,
pedicure, hairdressing, and, of course, facials.

Anne returned to the Raphael shortly before noon,
with over an hour to spare before her luncheon appointment with Paolo Martinelli. The citron cotton sheath she
had worn to Dragu Roma was now somewhat limp and
bedraggled, and she decided to change into the navy blue
suit Mario had expressed reserved approval of that first
night at dinner.

Suddenly she realized she would have to ask him for
a new outfit to wear this evening. She hated to impose
at such a busy time; still, only scant alterations had been
necessary on the aquamarine dress, and she wanted to
look her best for Justin. She knew just the dress she
wanted to wear—a ravishing off-the-shoulder taffeta
frock in several shades of blue and gray with a smocked,
drop-waisted skirt. Mario had shown the garment to her
yesterday as earmarked for her new wardrobe. Perhaps
the seamstress had already altered it; Mario had told her
the entire wardrobe would be sent to her hotel tomorrow
morning. With that cheering thought, Anne was starting
for the closet to get the navy suit when the phone rang.

"Anne! I've been trying to get you for hours." It was
Justin.

"I've been over at Dragu Roma," she explained,
amused that he should picture her riveted to her room at

the Raphael all morning in case he should call. "What's up?"

"Dragu Roma," he groaned. "That never occurred to me. I rang Mario and he said you weren't expected until lunchtime, and then I couldn't think where you might have gone. Listen, would it be possible for us to meet at a café in, say, twenty minutes—"

"No, it wouldn't be possible," Anne interrupted sharply. Her amusement at Justin's assumption that she should be constantly at his disposal had turned to irritation at his egotism. "My appointment with Paolo is for one fifteen."

There was a short silence on the other end. "All right then," Justin said. "I'd rather tell you this in person, but of course nothing must interfere with your grand appointment with Paolo."

"There's no need to be sarcastic," Anne told him huffily. "Now, what is it? I hope nothing's gone wrong betwen you and Signor Olivetti."

"No, no, nothing like that," he said dismissively, as if to imply that such a notion was ridiculous. "This has nothing to do with Marini or Dragu or any of the rest of it. Anne, have you seen a newspaper today?"

"No. Are the Red Brigades marching along the Appian Way?" she asked facetiously.

"Anne, this isn't funny. Listen. When I left Olivetti's today after picking up the contract drafts, I saw a headline on one of the tabloids . . ."

"Yes?" Anne prompted, mystified as to what Justin could possibly be leading up to. It wasn't like him to take so long to come to the point.

"Well, you remember my opera client, La Tiziana?" Without waiting for her to reply, he went on. "Apparently she took an overdose of sleeping pills in a suicide attempt last night. No reason given, though I have a hunch. Anyway, a maid found her in time and they pumped her stomach. But the thing is, I'll have to fly up to Milan this afternoon and see her as soon as possible."

"Is that really necessary?" Anne asked, upset at the prospect of Justin's sudden departure. "Can't you just telephone? If she's out of danger, I'm sure she has friends looking after her, and her manager—"

"Yes, yes, but you don't understand, Anne. Clarissa Stevens—that's her real name—is more than just a client. I knew her long before she repatriated to Italy and became La Tiziana."

"I suppose your families were old, old friends in New York?" Anne inquired acerbically. She knew she should be quiet and just let him explain, but she sensed that his explanation was only going to make matters worse.

"You're not making this any easier for me," he shot back. "I know I assured you I had never been involved with any of my clients, but this was so long ago that it hardly seemed to count and—"

"You were lovers!" Anne exclaimed, her heart in turmoil. He had lied to her. And if he'd lied about one woman, what about the rest?

"Listen, Anne, Clarissa was an undergraduate at Barnard when I was a law student at Columbia. We dated pretty steadily for several years. We even talked about marriage. I was the first guy she . . . went to bed with. That's all past history, of course, and this isn't the time to go into long explanations, but maybe now you can see why I have an obligation to go up there. She's very high-strung, and I'm one of the few people who knows how to handle her."

"I'll bet you do," Anne said sardonically.

"Anne, please, trust me. Look, let's not discuss it any more now. Take some time to think it over and cool off. I just called to tell you that I'm really sorry to cancel out on our date tonight, and I'll try to get back as soon as possible—tomorrow, I hope. I'll be in touch just as soon as I return, okay? And I'm bringing the Olivetti papers with me, so you can tell Marie she's not losing any of my time."

"Don't worry. I won't mention anything about anything to the countess," Anne said coldly. "As far as she'll know, you're still in Rome."

"Anne, I haven't been leading up to asking you to cover for me."

"Did I say you were? Justin, I have to go now. I think you may be right about a cooling-off period."

"Anne, just listen. With Clarissa, it was puppy love. With you—"

"Please, Justin. We'll talk when you get back." She didn't want to hear any more of his glib compliments.

"All right. Good-bye. Take care."

"Good-bye, Justin."

When she glanced at her watch as she hung up, she realized she was already late for her lunch appointment. Hurriedly she changed her dress and dashed to the hotel elevator. She had paid the taxi driver and was on the sidewalk in front of Casa Marini when she realized she'd forgotten to pick up the necklace from the hotel safe-deposit box. She hoped Mario would understand.

He did. "*Vedo*. Something has come up that has upset you. You will explain after your lunch with Paolo. Do not distress yourself any more about it."

Anne was amazed at the way she was able to keep her mind focused on the Marini line during her luncheon with the marketing manager. Like Mario, he was all graciousness and understanding about her tardiness, dismissing her vague apologies with, "You're here, *e basta*." She couldn't help but think how groundless Justin's suspicions about Paolo had been as he talked easily with her about wholesaling and retailing and pricing structures with the most professional of attitudes. But over coffee his mood changed suddenly, and Anne was appalled to hear him pouring out the story of his unhappy marriage.

"If only Italy were not a Catholic country," he lamented. "Giulia and I are divorced in spirit, divorced in the flesh, but in the Church. . . . We cannot scandalize the families, they are both very devout, and we have to think about our children also. However, we lead our own lives, I tell you that."

"I'm sure you're very sensible and civilized about your marriage, as you seem to be in general," Anne told him, accenting the adjectives and hoping the hint wasn't too subtle. "I think perhaps we'd better be getting back now, Paolo," she went on, trying to sound nonchalant. "I must say, it's been a very productive meeting. Thank you for the delicious meal."

Paolo was, after all, sensible and civilized, and took the squelching of his tentative overtures with good grace. "You are a very talented and interesting businesswoman," he said fluently. "It has been my pleasure."

When Anne returned to the salon, Mario was deep in conversation with an almost painfully thin woman. Exquisitely dressed, the client stood with an erect posture that only constant drilling from birth could have induced.

Mario beckoned Anne and performed the introductions.

"Anne, this is the Principessa de Beneditti. Principessa, Miss Anne Hopkins. Anne is taking Mario Marini to New York."

"To the world, Mario," Anne said, smiling. "How do you do, Principessa?"

"Quite well, thank you," the woman replied, examining Anne for a moment with frankly curious black eyes. "It is so unusual, Miss Hopkins, to find a woman in the business world. In Italy, that is." She sighed dramatically. "But then, poor Italy is so backward. We do not move with the times."

"No, Principessa," Mario said quickly, "we survive the times."

The Principessa emitted a shrill laugh. "Dear Mario. So amusing. And so talented. When you are a property of the world, I'm afraid we'll no longer see you in Rome."

"Desert you, Principessa? Never," the designer vowed quickly.

The principessa eyed Anne shrewdly. "And the charm of the man, my dear. You had better beware."

Anne smiled easily. "Ah, Principessa, I've already succumbed to the charm. After all, who could have resisted?"

The principessa looked a trifle startled. Still, Anne was pleased with herself for having held her own in the brittle exchange of banter, and for having found a way to thank Mario for the many courtesies he had shown her since her arrival in Rome.

"Indeed?" the principessa said, glancing from Anne to Mario and then back again with raised eyebrows. "I must go, Mario," she said abruptly. "Remember my party Friday night." In an afterthought she added, "Perhaps you would bring Miss Hopkins." She turned back toward Anne. "Everyone will want to meet you, my dear! Please do come."

After escorting the woman to the door, Mario returned to Anne and broke into laughter. Anne smiled at him questioningly.

Controlling himself, he explained, "From what you said, she is convinced that we are sleeping with one another."

"What? What did I say?" Anne wondered, alarmed.

"That you have succumbed to my charm."

"Oh, but I didn't mean . . . I mean, I didn't think . . . I mean, I meant I *liked* you."

"I know, I know, Annina. But di Benedetti's daughter, Angela, is one of my best clients, and a close friend of Monica Arletti's. The principessa will gossip to Angela, and Angela will repeat the gossip to Monica. And Monica will eat her heart out. Perhaps," he added wistfully, "she will come back to me."

Anne was torn between compassion for him and uneasiness for herself. Mario must have seen the dismay in her eyes, for he said immediately, "Ah, but I have been thinking only of myself. You are distressed that these rumors will get back to your Signor Bradley."

"He's not my Signor Bradley," Anne said sadly. "Now less than ever." Briefly she told him about La Tiziana's attempted suicide, Justin's confession, and his sudden departure.

"Annina," Mario said gently, "you are wrong to be angry with him. His loyalty and compassion do him credit. With the first love—when there is no anger and bitterness in the parting—there is often a lasting *tenerezza*, a tenderness. I know. There was a girl in Napoli, she was my childhood sweetheart. But she did not want to come to Rome, I did not want to stay in Naples, and we realized we wanted different things out of life. She is married now, with four children. But when I visit my parents, I always go to see her, and if—God forbid—something like this should happen to Giovanna, I would fly to her side at once."

"You would?" Anne asked in a small voice.

"But *certo*. Now, Signor Bradley is coming back when?"

Anne shrugged. "He said he hoped tomorrow, but I wouldn't be surprised if he decided to stay for the weekend."

"It is possible, that," Mario mused. "But you must occupy yourself in the meantime, not give over to brooding. It would be a very good thing for you to attend this party of the principessa's on Friday night. There will be people there you should meet. She has invited you to accompany me. You will do me the honor?"

"Thank you, Mario. Yes, I will go with you." She

knew the countess would want her to attend this soirée.

"*Benissimo*. It is settled. Wait till you see the gown I will select for you to wear. I will send the wardrobe over tomorrow, as I said. You can send the necklace back with my man. Or no, bring it back yourself, and we will have lunch together. *D'accordo?*"

"Thank you, Mario. I'll see you at one."

"In the little taffeta frock that you so much admired, *sì?*"

"*Sì,*" Anne repeated tonelessly, remembering how she had looked forward to wearing that very frock this evening with Justin.

- 8 -

ANNE DUTIFULLY CALLED the countess after returning to her hotel from Casa Marini. The old woman was delighted to hear from her and said so emphatically. She also had Anne repeat several times the details of her various conversations with Mario and the report on the Rome salon.

"I like your idea of partitioning the facial rooms and sales boutique of Dragu Roma into mini-Marini sections," the countess enthused. "Mother and daughter can go together and chat while they're each getting their own new look. You'll have to take it up with Signora Gemini and her people, of course, but you may tell them I approve. Now, what are Marini's ideas for the new cosmetics line?"

"I don't know," Anne confessed. "As I told you, we're going to get together early next week to discuss that."

"When?"

"Well, we didn't make a definite date . . ."

"Make one!" the old woman ordered. "Get over there tomorrow and pin him down. Now, I'm sure everything will be all right, Anne. I have every confidence in you. But Justin has to know what he's talking about with

Maestro Olivetti. Speaking of Justin, what's he up to?"

"He's studying some preliminary contract drafts Maestro Olivetti worked up based on their discussions so far," Anne replied half-truthfully. "By the way, he knows Marini's top model and—"

"Yes, yes, he told me all about it," the countess broke in. "You know," she added, "that gives me an idea. The best news you've had for me is that Marini's letting his models do their own makeup for the showing. It would have been rather awkward if he'd signed a contract with one of our competitors for that. Now, I think it would be wise for Justin to speak to his little friend about using Dragu products, and she could then talk the other models into doing likewise."

"That's an excellent idea," Anne said, wishing she had thought of it herself. Still, she was none too pleased at the prospect of Justin dining with Monica Arletti again. She wasn't totally convinced that the beautiful model wasn't setting her cap for Justin after all as the path of least resistance to please her parents.

"Good, I'll call him—no, I won't. You tell him," the countess ordered, "and have him call me and report on the matter. One phone call is cheaper than two. Harumph, where were we? Oh, yes. Anne, I want you to nail down that meeting with Marini about the new line and call me back as soon as you can tell me about it. Is that understood?"

"Yes, Countess." They talked for a few more minutes, the old woman advising Anne to visit some of her competitors' salons and see what they were up to, and also to look around at the boutique and department store cosmetics displays.

"I want you to get a sense of perspective about the differences between New York and the Continent," the countess told her. "I may be sending you out on the international circuit more. I need a younger person to do some of that jetting around and checking on my salons abroad for me."

"Yes, Countess." Anne felt her spirits soar. She had feared the countess had been displeased with her over her failure to get down to brass tacks with Mario about the new line, but apparently the old woman was satisfied with her after all.

It wasn't until early evening, as she was roaming aimlessly about the Forum, determined to drink in more of the ancient Roman splendors with or without Justin, that Anne again turned her thoughts to her telephone conversation with him. As her eyes wandered over the scattered columns in a plethora of styles and the scarred and battered triumphal arches, she asked herself if she had, as Mario implied, been overhasty in condemning Justin. The crux of the matter was whether his rushing to the diva's side had truly been motivated by a sense of obligation to a distant past, and whether the fact that he had been less than totally truthful about the matter meant he had been altogether duplicitous with her.

Seating herself on a fragment of fluted column and plucking one of the acanthus leaves that ran rampant around the scattered stones, Anne marshaled the evidence for herself. Justin had said he had an idea why the opera singer had attempted suicide—could it be something that had occurred between them during his sojourn in Milan the previous week? But the motive might have had nothing whatsoever to do with Justin; the woman obviously confided in him.

Twirling the acanthus leaf between her thumb and forefinger, Anne realized the flimsiness of the evidence on which she had been ready to believe Justin was still carrying on with his old flame.

But that still left the question of his honesty. Perhaps La Tiziana was not the only former lover among his clientele. Yet what real reason did she have to believe that? Wasn't she only trying to believe the worst of Justin because she was afraid of losing her heart to him?

Discarding the acanthus leaf, Anne rose and began to walk in the direction of a ruined circular temple that she recognized from her guidebook as the Temple of the Vestal Virgins. Reading the brochure in the taxi on her way to the Via dei Fori Imperiali, she had been both fascinated and appalled at the idea that young women would sign a thirty-year contract to remain virgins while guarding the sacred flame of the goddess of the hearth. Those priestesses who broke their holy vows were buried alive, but transgressors had apparently been few, and most of the vestals had elected to remain immured for life in what had then been a rich marble dwelling two stories high.

Now, standing in the atrium of the ruin along with a crowd of other tourists, Anne wondered if the vestals had not chosen the better part after all. They'd had many more privileges than the other women of their day and lived in splendor; nor did they lack for female companionship. Yet they had sacrificed love and passion, marriage and children.

Unbidden, the sensation of Justin's lips on hers and his electric fingers caressing her skin came back to her, and she trembled. The vestal virgins might have made the wiser choice and spared themselves a lot of heartache by their decision, but Anne knew she could never have followed such a path.

The fact of the matter was, she admitted to herself, she was falling in love with Justin Bradley.

- 9 -

FIRST THING THURSDAY morning the hotel desk rang Anne to inform her that her wardrobe had been delivered from Casa Marini. As she carefully hung up the assortment of colorful dresses and smart pantsuits, casual wear, cocktail dresses, and the magnificent black lace gown Mario had chosen for her to wear to the principessa's, she felt the despondency that had clung to her since the previous evening begin to lift.

Walking from the Forum to the Campidoglio, Anne had finally acknowledged to herself that she had wronged Justin by her suspicions. She began to fear he would return from Milan alienated and resentful, and ready to turn his attentions elsewhere. Doubtless there were plenty of women in Rome who would love to go out with him. Her heart contracted with pain at the thought of him with another woman.

But now, as she surveyed the array of stylish new garments in her closet, she felt her confidence return. She would look her best when she next saw Justin; she would inquire sympathetically after his friend; and she would admit that she had acted like a jealous harpy and was sorry. Justin was sensitive. He would understand and forgive. But would he love her?

Anne wished fervently that she hadn't cut him off on

97

the phone when he started to say what he felt for her. At the time she had thought he was merely trying to appease her with flattery. Now she wondered if she hadn't nipped in the bud a declaration that might never come again.

At ten o'clock she set forth to visit some of the cosmetics salons in Mario's vicinity and to make purchases and comparisons so the countess could be fully informed about her competition. She stopped first at Mario's salon to return the necklace and found him in the midst of a fitting with Monica. It was the first time the two American women had come face-to-face since their initial meeting at the Sans Souci, and Anne couldn't help noticing that Monica's hostility, which had been focused primarily on Mario that evening, now encompassed her as well.

Monica looked daggers when Anne told Mario she was returning the necklace. The daggers grew sharper when Mario alluded to their date for the principessa's soirée the following evening. Yet Anne wasn't disturbed by Monica's obvious jealousy. If the model still cared so much about Mario, it was unlikely she would throw herself at Justin. Or was it? Perhaps Monica would seek to forget the old love by flinging herself into a new romance.

Later, after her morning of comparison shopping, Anne broached the subject to Mario over lunch in what he described as a *"tavèrna tìpica romana."* As they attacked their hearty veal steaks drenched in a sauce of sage and butter, Anne remarked, "Your campaign to make Monica jealous seems to be having some effect."

"Yes, a great effect." He gloated. "She has been talking to her friend Angela, and she is burning with *gelosìa*. She thought I would finally come crawling to her, saying I would wait forever, if necessary, for her parents' blessing on our engagement. But no, it is Monica who will come crawling to me, you will see, and soon."

"How can you be sure she won't try to turn the tables?" Anne asked tentatively.

"Monica use another man to make me jealous? No, I don't believe it. At first that was what I thought she was doing with Signor Bradley, but now I see I was mistaken. She went out with him only because she knew the old family friend wouldn't make a pass at her. With other men she could not be so sure, and it is me she loves. Oh, she will flirt madly at the principessa's party, but never too long with one man, and only when I am nearby to observe her. And then, perhaps the next morning, with a long weekend stretching ahead of her, she will call and humbly beg my forgiveness." Mario's roguish features spread into a delighted grin.

"Ah—speaking of the weekend, Mario, will you find time to work on some conceptions for the Marini cosmetics line?" Anne asked, mindful of the countess's injunction.

"Yes, yes, of course. I have promised you and I will do that."

"Fine," she replied. "Then why don't we set up a meeting for Monday?"

He took a sip of his Chianti and considered. "I tell you what, Annina. Next week, every day I will be running around like a chicken without its head making final preparations for the showing of my collection. Why don't we meet Monday evening? I hope you understand that I will be too exhausted for a long dinner, but perhaps you could drop over at my apartment around nine, nine-thirty, and I will give you a little supper as we talk. There is a pizzeria near me. I will have them send up one of their specialties, a lasagna pizza. I'll bet you never had such a thing in America."

"Never," Anne confirmed. "Lasagna pizza? It sounds scrumptious."

"Scrumptious?" Mario's brow furrowed in puzzlement.

"Delicious. Good to eat," Anne explained.

"Ah. Scrumptious." He looked thoughtful. "I like that word. It suggests possibilities to me. So, it is settled about Monday evening?"

"Yes. I'll need your address, though."

"Of course. I will write it down for you." He whipped out a small address book, tore out a sheet of paper, and made a few scrawls on it.

Anne looked at the piece of paper. "The Via dei Monti. That's near the church, Trinità dei Monti?"

"Right. On the other side of the Piazza di Spagna from my salon. You will tell the taxi driver. He will know where to take you."

"Thank you, Mario. I'll be looking forward to that lasagna pizza."

"And to hearing my proposals for the Marini line of cosmetics?" he asked with a twinkle in his black eyes. "Do not distress yourself, Annina, you will be satisfied, I guarantee it."

When Anne returned to her hotel in the late afternoon, there were two messages that Signor Bradley had called, once in the morning and again about an hour before. He had left no number where he could be reached. Anne's heart sank. Justin must be planning to extend his stay in Milan.

But when he finally reached her by phone in the evening, as she was preparing to go down to the hotel dining room for a solitary dinner, he told her he was back in Rome. "I tried to get you to give you my flight time," he explained. "I wanted to make sure you hadn't made other plans for the evening."

"I've made no plans," Anne said simply, her pulse racing in anticipation of seeing him.

"Good. Shall I pick you up in half an hour? We can

go to that place in Trastevere I told you about."

"I'll wait for you at the sleigh," she promised.

Since she had complied with Mario's request that she wear the taffeta frock for their luncheon, she now had to change into something else for her date with Justin. But with a splendid new wardrobe to choose from, she didn't mind. Ultimately she chose an elegant sheath of rich forest-green velvet. The material was butter-soft and clung to every curve of her body, while a wide gilt belt set off her waist. The rather short skirt also showed her legs to advantage, and she thought Justin would like the high gold-sequin-trimmed collar that stood up stiffly around the neck like a queen's ruff. He seemed to fancy her in the role of Guinevere, and the collar was a quaint contrast to the plunging neckline, with its scalloped border of gold sequins.

When she saw Justin waiting for her by the antique sleigh, Anne forgot her own appearance, she was so captivated by his. His three-piece white linen suit was debonair and elegant, and his bright-yellow tie added just the right touch of color, as well as emphasizing the golden flecks in his eyes. His whole face lit up when he saw her, and her pulses quickened with hope. Then she felt a moment's panic. Suppose his admiration was only for her outfit?

But as he gathered her silently into his arms and pressed her passionately against his long length, she was reassured. When they separated, he said simply, "I've missed you, Anne," and the expression in his eyes told her how much.

Relief flooded through her, followed by exhilaration. He wasn't angry, and he still cared for her! She stifled simultaneous urges to laugh hysterically and burst into tears. There was a noticeable catch in her voice as she replied, "I've missed you, too."

"I brought you a present from Milan," he said. Taking

her hand, he led her to one of the overstuffed couches in the lobby. "Sit down and I'll give it to you."

"A present?" she asked, her face warm with excitement. What could he have brought?

When she opened the slim box that he withdrew from an inside pocket of his jacket, she saw it was an ankle bracelet—a delicate gold chain surrounded a wider gold band that was ornamented with the raised figure of a medieval knight on horseback on the left side, and a garland of hearts and flowers on the right side.

"Justin, how exquisite," she breathed. "I've never seen anything like it."

"I thought of you the minute I saw it in the shop window," he said, smiling enchantingly. "I remembered how in the days of Camelot it was the custom for knights to give some token to their ladies—" He broke off, embarrassed. "Does it sound too corny to say I wanted to give it to you as a token?"

"Justin, I'm so moved," she said tremulously. "I don't know what to say."

"How about asking me to put it on for you?" he teased.

Wordlessly she lifted her right leg, and he stooped and fastened the bracelet around her ankle. "It suits you perfectly," he said proudly. "I was sure it would."

Anne was inordinately pleased with his gift. It was unabashedly romantic, and she glowed at the image of him dashing impetuously into some shop in Milan to buy it for her.

"I'll treasure it always," she promised with a solemn note in her voice that surprised her. "I really don't know how to thank you."

"Just keep looking at me with that soft light in your eyes," he said in a low voice. "That's all the thanks I want."

They exchanged a look of tenderness and longing that surpassed anything they could have expressed in words.

Then Justin rose and he held out his arm to escort her from the hotel.

They spoke little in the taxi on the way to the restaurant. Anne was content to nestle silently in Justin's arms as he held her close and pushed back her wavy curtain of burnished hair to cover her neck and shoulders with dozens of light, butterfly kisses. From time to time she glanced at the gleaming gold of the ankle bracelet, and the sight filled her with a warm radiance. Once Justin reached down and gave the ornament a proprietary caress—but no, Anne realized, the caress was for her ankle. With leisurely grace he let his fingers wander up the length of her calf, sending an arrow of flame to her very core. His hand continued upward to lightly stroke her thigh with a voluptuous motion that made her moan with passion.

It was all the invitation he needed. His arms crushed her to his chest, and his scalding lips swooped down on hers with predatory hunger. Delicious sensations coursed through her veins as she captured his tongue with hers, and they savored each other's sweetness.

"You taste so good" he murmured, licking first one earlobe and then the other in a way that drove her wild.

"Better than a *monte bianco*?" she teased.

He laughed. "I refuse to be sidetracked, *carissima*," he growled with mock severity as his mouth kissed a path along her cheek to her lips.

"Why *carissima*?" she wondered aloud when he returned again to her earlobes.

"Because it means the sweetest of sweethearts—which is how I feel about you," he said gruffly, pulling a long strand of her flame-colored hair across his lips and kissing it inch by inch. "English endearments just aren't emphatic enough." He nuzzled her neck tenderly with his tongue. "Mmm," he sighed. *"Carissima, bellissima, amorissima."*

"There's no such word as *amorissima*," she said reproachfully. "Justin, you're pulling my leg."

"No, I'm caressing it," he said, and proceeded to do so again. "There is too such a word—I just made it up. It means loveliest of loves."

Anne laughed, delighted. "Justin, you're full of yourself just because you have a way with words."

"Ah, but when will I have my way with you?" he murmured devilishly as his fingers feathered their way boldly up her thigh. "No, don't answer that. Surprise me," he said with a rakish chuckle.

"Signor, signorina, here is the Vìcolo di Santa Maria in Trastevere," the cabdriver broke into their intimacy as they pulled into a narrow street just off the bohemian quarter's main piazza.

"Wouldn't you know?" Justin said, relinquishing her ruefully and reaching into his pocket for his wallet.

Apparently in gratitude for the generous tip, the taxi driver urged them cordially to enjoy their dinner and gave Justin a broad wink. He returned the wink, then helped Anne out of the car with characteristic attentiveness.

The restaurant, Sabatini's, consisted of several tavern-style dining rooms with wide arches, beamed ceilings, and fanciful wall frescoes. After the maître d' had seated them, they studied the predominantly seafood menu in silence, Justin managing to hold his with one hand while the other hand found Anne's knee under the table.

As appetizers Anne ordered *zuppa di cozze*, a savory mussel stew, and Justin an antipasto *misto mare*, a smorgasbord of fruits of the sea. Although his hand remained proprietarily on her knee as they sipped their wine and waited for their food, Anne felt a sudden shyness descend inexplicably over both of them.

"How was your friend when you saw her, Justin?" she asked hesitantly.

"A little rocky, as you might expect under the circumstances," he answered slowly, "but the nurse said she was recuperating rapidly."

"She was in the hospital then?"

"No, Clarissa has a horror of hospitals, thinks they're bad for the voice. She was at her apartment, under the care of a private nurse."

"How was she emotionally?" Anne ventured quietly.

"Alternately despondent and manic, but that's Clarissa's personality," he explained. "It was as I thought, a problem in her love life. For the past year she's been having an affair with a wealthy Milan industrialist who's quite a bit older than she is. He's a widower with no children, and recently he's been threatening to marry someone else unless Clarissa retires from the stage and gives him an heir. Well, it seems he finally made good on his threat, and she read of his engagement in *Corriere della Sera*. She hoped her suicide attempt would bring him flying to her side."

"But it brought you instead? I'm sorry, Justin," she apologized immediately. "I didn't mean to sound peevish."

His face creased into dimples. "But I like it when you're jealous. Maybe it shows you're beginning to care for me just a little?" He bent his head to try to see her lowered eyes. "But to get back to Clarissa," he went on, chuckling to himself, "no, her boyfriend didn't come running. Guess he'd made up his mind."

"He didn't even call? That must have been devastating for her," Anne said with genuine sympathy.

"He did send flowers, but the note only said, 'It's too late.' That seemed to anger her. 'È *tarde*, he tells me,' she said, waving the note at me. 'È *tarde*,—just like Violetta in the last act of *Traviata*. Doesn't he know that's *my* line? All the critics write that I say it even more movingly than Callas did.'

"I'm not trying to make her grief sound comical, Anne,

but with Clarissa even moments of genuine emotion become melodrama. Part of her is always playing the role of tragedy queen. The problem is, she wants it all. She's determined to be the operatic superstar of the century, with flocks of adoring fans sleeping outside the box office to get tickets for her performances. Obviously that kind of career leaves little time for family life, or even the kind of commitment it takes to make a relationship work. But she can't understand when her lovers desert her. She expects them to accommodate all their needs and desires to her legend."

"Is that what happened between you?" Anne asked sympathetically as their waiter set their appetizers before them and departed.

Justin toyed with his food before answering. "More or less, although Clarissa wasn't a legend in those days, only an aspiring one. She was in her last year at Barnard and had just been accepted for graduate study in voice at Juilliard when we met. I was in my first year of law school and had never been seriously in love before."

"How did you meet?" Anne wondered. "Isn't the Columbia campus pretty large?"

"It is, but I always had my eye peeled for an attractive woman," Justin confessed sheepishly. "Anyway, one day I was walking down Columbus Avenue and I saw this wonderful mane of flaming hair streaming in the wind before me. I followed her to a restaurant and managed to wangle permission to join her for lunch. I was so smitten, it wasn't until long afterward that I realized she had totally monopolized the conversation that afternoon. At the time I was content to listen and adore."

"I know what you mean," Anne said truthfully, remembering how it had been with Chuck.

"On our next date I let her know I had sung at the Met," he recalled with a grin. "I'll never forget how her face fell when I explained that I was only an extra there.

But after that she was always pumping me for backstage anecdotes about various singers. When I couldn't remember any more, I began inventing them—nothing slanderous, of course, but outrageous enough to keep Clarissa amused."

Anne laughed with him. "I have a feeling all the adoration wasn't on your side," she said. "Surely Clarissa wasn't immune to your charm."

"I didn't mean to imply it was totally one-sided," he admitted. "We were infatuated with each other, although sometimes I felt she cared more for the externals—the fact that I'm from an old family, had been to Europe often as a child, that kind of thing. Then, too, there was the physical side of it."

Silence hung between them. "When did her singing start to come between you?" Anne asked finally.

"Well, from the beginning the voice came first. I could understand and even sympathize with her ambitions, but I hoped we could marry and work things out. I wasn't ready for children yet myself and was realistic about the fact that there might be long stretches when we couldn't be together. But I figured I could become her attorney and acquire a roster of other operatic clients, so that might minimize the separations."

"And so you proposed," Anne prodded him, feeling an irrational stab of jealousy.

"And so I proposed," he repeated. "I even literally went down on my knees, knowing how Clarissa would appreciate the grand gesture. It was wasted effort, though. She said she would always have a special place for me in her heart but she was now at a turning point in her career. Like many young American singers, she found the opportunities for native talent limited and had decided to try her luck abroad. I asked her to wait a year, until I had finished law school, but she was adamant.

"I was devastated," he went on. "I thought she loved

me, and when she rejected me with no apparent qualms or inner conflict—well, it hurt like hell. I've never acknowledged that before, Anne. Maybe the reason I didn't tell you, or anyone else, about my relationship with Clarissa is that I didn't want to admit that I'd ever been burned."

Anne had thought of Justin as a man who completely dominated women, seeing him so vulnerable, knowing he had experienced the same anguish and sense of abandonment she had felt when Chuck left, created a new bond of closeness with him.

Impulsively she reached across the table and took his hand, conveying her empathy with a gentle caress over his long, tapering fingers.

His face cleared and he smiled at her. "Do you know that's the first time you've done that? I mean, the first time you've touched me without my making the first move."

Anne smiled shyly at him and gave his hand a gentle squeeze.

Their fingers interlaced, he continued, "I suppose after that you wonder how I came to be Clarissa's attorney."

She looked at him encouragingly.

"Well, she went abroad and almost immediately made it into the big European houses. I followed her progress in the newspaper reviews, and I began to realize she had probably done me a big favor by refusing to marry me. I'm very possessive, and I wouldn't have wanted to share her with the world.

"I never expected to see her again this side of the footlights. But one day she showed up at the firm, giving the receptionist a hard time and demanding to see me instantly. It seemed she'd just fired her umpteenth lawyer and had been reading about me in *The New York Times*, which she continued to buy in Europe—homesickness, I guess."

"When was this?" Anne asked.

"About five years ago. She was anxious to have a good lawyer because the Met was finally showing some interest in her, although ultimately it came to nothing because she didn't like the roles they offered her."

"Wasn't it painful to see her again?" Anne inquired compassionately.

"Only during the first few minutes of shock and nostalgia. She'd changed. She had become a demanding, hysterical, and almost megalomaniacal tyrant. Only in that silvery laughter of hers, and her complete dedication to her art, was there any vestige of the Clarissa I had loved. And by then I had my own career, and I realized all that wouldn't have been possible if I'd married her. I would have been nothing more than a sort of stage prop in her life. She even told me that she was grateful to me for teaching her to play a woman in love convincingly. That's all our relationship meant to her—something to use in her singing."

"Yet you became close again?" Anne persisted, wanting to know the truth of their relationship.

"In a different way. At the time I began representing her, Clarissa was beginning to experience vocal troubles. She had taken on too many demanding roles too soon, and her voice, which is very light, couldn't take the strain. Opera's a very opportunistic world, and when her voice became uneven, not only did the offers stop coming in from the major houses, but her so-called friends deserted her. I became her confidant, holding her hand and assuring her that if she gave her voice ample rest and stuck to the lighter repertoire, it would all come back. Sure enough, within a year her voice was fine. She was grateful to me—she said without my support she never would have had the confidence to go on."

"There was never any temptation for either of you to become lovers again?"

He shook his head. "There were other men in her life and other women in mine. Clarissa could easily acquire lovers. What she needed was a friend. She told me yesterday that I was her only true friend."

"And what did you say to her?" Anne asked, satisfied that he was no longer in love with the diva.

"Oh, I fanned her ego, reminded her how much she meant to her public, and pointed out that next year she'll finally be fulfilling her dream of singing at the Met on her terms. I told her there'd be other men, as I'm sure there will be, that she was in her prime and more beautiful than ever. And I got her to sing for me, as she used to do in our student days. Nothing cheers Clarissa up like letting loose with a grand, self-pitying aria."

They were silent as the waiter cleared away their half-eaten appetizers and brought on the main course, grilled fish.

"So," Justin said softly, pouring them each another glass of wine, "I've told you my story. Do you think you can tell me yours now?"

She had dreaded telling him about Chuck, but now that he had shared so much with her, she found it wasn't as painful as she'd imagined. Justin gazed into her eyes sympathetically as she explained how Chuck's good looks and sophistication had swept her off her feet.

"I thought the fact that we were both in the business world would be a bond between us," she said. "But it didn't work out that way." She told him how Chuck's interest seemed to wane when she went back to school for her M.B.A. and how he had betrayed her with his secretary.

"Perhaps his own career wasn't taking off as quickly as he'd expected," Justin suggested. "Television is a very competitive field. Chuck must have felt threatened by your success at Dragu. He was probably terrified that one day you were going to surpass him careerwise. He didn't have to worry about that with his secretary."

"I don't know," Anne said, taking a sip of wine. "He left so abruptly. All I could think was, what did I do wrong? At least with Clarissa you knew it wasn't *you*."

"It wasn't *you* either, Anne," he said hotly, as he placed a supportive hand on her knee under the table and gave it a light caress. "Chuck's own insecurity was the problem. Don't you realize what an incredibly desirable woman you are? Beautiful, bright, easy to talk to..."

Anne sighed. "It was just so shattering to suddenly find myself deserted. Alone."

His golden-brown eyes looked meaningfully into hers. "You're not alone now." His voice was soothing and at the same time seductive.

"I'm afraid," she admitted softly.

"Still? After all we've shared tonight? I feel so close to you, so... connected. I want you in my life, darling. I want you so much it hurts."

But will you always feel that way? Anne's heart screamed silently.

As if guessing her feelings, he took her hand and kissed each fingertip lightly, lovingly. "*Amorissima,* trust me."

She was spared from answering by the approach of their waiter. "You have barely touched the fish!" he protested when Justin motioned for the check. "And most of the appetizers, too, were left uneaten. *Signor, sinorina,* Sabatini's is one of the finest seafood restaurants in all Italy? What am I to think?"

His outrage seemed so out of proportion that Anne had to smile. But she found herself tongue-tied before the elderly man's indignation.

"You are to think only that love takes away the appetite," Justin said easily, giving the white-haired waiter a dazzling smile. "And that is no reflection on the well-deserved reputation of Sabatini's."

Under the spell of Justin's winsome compliment, the old man's stern features relaxed. He beamed at them. "So you are in love. I am an old man. I forget the power of the feelings. But I wish you joy. You are young, you are free. Be happy."

In Italian it sounded like a benediction. Yet to Anne the words also seemed to carry a note of warning: *be happy with Justin before the moment is lost.* She waited expectantly for her inner demon to protest, but the voice that echoed in her heart was Justin's: *"Amorissima, trust me."* Her entire being was filled with a lambent glow.

She seemed to float out of the restaurant on Justin's arm, conscious only of the new intimacy between them and the love token he had placed on her ankle.

A taxi was waiting in the street. "I'm going back to the Raphael with you tonight, Anne," Justin said with quiet authority as he opened the car door for her.

Where was the fear, the panic? She felt only delicious anticipation and longing. "We are young, we are free, we will be happy," she echoed the waiter's words, and sealed the promise with a kiss that lasted until the cab pulled up before the entrance to her hotel.

Justin held her hand in a firm clasp as they walked through the foyer and took the elevator to her room. Anne felt acutely conscious of every movement she made, of every sight and sound she encountered. Time seemed to be suspended in a haze of delicious anticipation of the moment when Justin would take her into his arms.

After locking the door of her suite behind them, he scooped her up in his masterful arms and carried her wordlessly into the bedroom lowering her gently, like a precious treasure, onto the quilt-covered bed.

"Anne, Anne, my wonderful, precious, luscious Anne," he whispered hoarsely as his fingers lovingly memorized the contours of her face and throat in the velvety darkness of the room.

"Justin." She ran her fingers through the soft waves of his hair.

He bent his head and planted a moist kiss on the hollow of her throat, then another between her breasts. Her fingers found the satiny skin on the back of his neck, and she felt a tremor of longing go through him at her caress.

The fierce urgency of his kiss confirmed his yearning. Anne felt an answering ache in herself. As their tongues plundered one another's honeyed mouths, she felt the sinewy muscles of his long limbs strain against her yielding curves.

"I want you so," he said, breathing heavily as he unzipped her dress to the waist and his hands skimmed over the lacy fabric of her bra, teasing the nipples that hardened and rose to his touch.

"So sweet," he murmured, rolling the swollen buds gently between his fingers. As the movement became more frenzied, a torch ignited inside her, and she gave a low moan. With practiced ease he unfastened her bra, and then his tongue replaced his hands as he laved deft, fiery circles around the peaks.

She was all feeling, all delicious, euphoric sensation, as he flicked the swollen nipples with his burning tongue. His hands found their way beneath her skirt and stroked her sensitive inner thighs, sending jolts of ecstasy through her flesh beneath the sheer covering of her stockings.

She was barely conscious of the involuntary groans that came from her throat as he continued to explore her half-clothed body for what seemed an eternity of pleasure. Boldly she let her hand travel up his thigh to rest on his male desire, both astonished and pleased at her own temerity. She forgot all modesty in the desire to return intimacy for intimacy, pleasure for pleasure.

"I love the way you touch me," he whispered as he began to pluck away her dress, half slip, ankle bracelet, and stockings, like the petals of a flower. When she protested, "I want to wear it," he reclasped the bracelet over her bare skin.

He took his time undressing her, evoking ever greater raptures with the kisses and caresses he placed on each new area he uncovered. She was deeply moved by his tenderness and concern for her. She had never known it could be like this . . .

She wanted to discover every delight of his body as well. With trembling hands she found his belt buckle and unfastened it. The linen slacks slipped easily over his lean hips, and her fingertips grazed wonderingly over his long, muscular legs. The buttons on his shirt came undone with quicksilver speed, and now they were both completely naked, exploring each other's most sensitive places first with infinite tenderness, then with mounting passion.

The intensity of her arousal was becoming unbearable. Finally he lifted himself over her and their bodies came together in an electric contact of skin on skin. She felt a warm, wet gliding as they attained the ultimate intimacy. Anne marveled at the way she seemed to open to him like a morning glory to the dawn, and then she lost all separate sense of herself as they moved together as one in an ageless rhythm.

Reveling in their mysterious union, she clasped her hands behind his neck, and his tongue parted her lips for a ravishing kiss. She was completely filled with him as she instinctively matched his thrusts, bringing him deeper and deeper inside her.

Their bodies taking them on an ever-wilder journey, he murmured love words in her ear and she responded with her own endearments. He lifted her from plane to higher plane of sensuality. She had never known such pleasure, never dreamed such an absolute feeling of wholeness with another person was possible.

His burning lips were at the curve of her neck, behind

her ears, on her forehead. "You're so silky, so perfect," he gasped as she tightened around him and the pace of their movements quickened.

Murmuring an endless litany of endearments, he brought her to the edge of the universe, and together they floated into paradise in a shuddering, ecstatic release. Anne felt utterly complete and at peace.

They lay quietly, still joined, as the wondrous sensations gradually dissipated, the rainbows faded and vanished, and their breathing returned to normal.

"Anne, my own Anne. My own, own Anne, now and for all time," Justin breathed reverently, raining kisses on her forehead, eyelids, and chin.

"Justin. *Carissimo, amorissimo.*" Anne felt her feelings couldn't be adequately expressed in any language. She had never experienced such bliss, such utter serenity and fulfillment.

He hugged the small of her back, and his tongue began a game of hide and seek with hers. As they luxuriated in their supreme intimacy, Anne felt Justin grow hard again inside her.

"Oh!" she murmured in surprise as his hips began to gyrate above her.

He gave a low chuckle. "Making up for lost time, my loveliest of loves."

She was even more startled when he switched on the bedside wall light. "I want to look at you," he explained, thrusting further into her.

The second time was more tender, less frantic, but the final rapture was equally shattering. Again Anne was conscious of transcending all earthly bounds as she soared with Justin to a celestial sphere where all was light and color and unalloyed bliss.

As they lay side by side, Justin nuzzled her stomach playfully, licking her navel and tickling her sides until she shrieked, "Uncle!" between gales of laughter.

"Sex makes you very ticklish," he commented, his eyes twinkling with mischief. "I'll have to remember that."

"And what about you?" Catching him off guard, she ran her fingers in a titillating motion across the matted hair of his underarm, then teasingly tweaked his nipples until he squirmed in laughing surrender.

"Enough!" he gasped. "Enough."

Anne imagined a youthful, roguish Justin superimposed on the incredibly handsome man who lay at her mercy.

"You're as sneaky as my sister Carol," he accused her lightly.

"I didn't know you had a sister. Older or younger?" Suddenly Anne wanted to know everything about him.

"I have two sisters, both older. Redheads, like my mother." Catching a strand of her gleaming hair and raising it to his lips, he added with a grin, "You can guess what a Freudian would make of that. But don't you believe it. I love you for yourself."

"What?" Were the sweet words only part of his teasing?

"I love you." This time he said it worshipfully, and there could be no doubt of his sincerity.

Her heart jumped to her throat. "Justin."

"Justin, what?"

"Justin, I love you."

"Again."

"I love you." As she repeated the words, she realized how truly she meant them.

"And I love you, my own Anne."

"Justin, it was so...so..." Words failed her.

"I know. For me, too."

"But..."

"Never like that. Never with any other woman," he answered the question in her eyes.

"I wish tonight would never end," she said dreamily.

"It won't. We won't let it. Tomorrow's Friday. We'll cancel all our appointments," he said recklessly. "And then the whole weekend will be one glorious continuation of tonight."

She sighed contentedly, then suddenly remembered. Tomorrow night was the principessa's soirée! She'd promised Mario . . .

"It will be our weekend," Justin continued happily. "We'll have breakfast in bed, lunch in bed, dinner in bed. Prisoners of love . . ."

"Justin . . ."

"Don't look so alarmed, Anne. Don't you know when I'm kidding? Of course we'll fit in some sightseeing. We'll go to the Keats house tomorrow, okay? And then tomorrow night—"

"About tomorrow night," she began guardedly.

"What about it? Would you prefer a disco, or the opera, or a moonlit stroll around Rome?"

He was so romantic, so tender, she didn't know how to tell him about the principessa's party. Perhaps if she was casual about it . . .

"The good news," she began brightly, "is that we have all of Saturday and Sunday together. The bad news is that tomorrow night Mario—"

"Mario," Justin repeated, frowning. "Good lord, Anne, don't tell me you made plans with Mario for a Friday night. I know he's an important client, but I'm sure he'll understand if you reschedule your meeting for next week. You can take him to lunch somewhere spiffy."

"I can't reschedule this, Justin."

"Can't?" His eyebrows shot up in surprise and indignation. "You mean you made a *date* with Mario? While I was in Milan—"

"That's just the point. You were in Milan, and I wasn't sure you'd be back for the weekend."

"I told you on the phone I'd be back tonight!" His voice shook with anger.

"You said you *hoped* you would," she reminded him. "Listen, Justin, it's not what you think. I don't have a 'date' with Mario. He offered to escort me to a soirée given by the Principessa di Benedetti. He says there will be people there I should meet. I'm sure the countess would want me to go. And Mario might be offended if I back out."

"Well, I'll be offended if you don't!" he exploded. "Whose feelings are more important to you, Anne— mine or Mario's?"

"Justin, that isn't the issue. Remember, this is a business engagement."

"Business engagement!" he scoffed. "I've been to more than one of these high-society Roman parties myself, and I know exactly how much *business* goes on at them. Anne, you've been invited to a damn orgy. And Mario knows it."

She was genuinely shocked. "Justin, Mario is a gentleman. He would never—"

"Wouldn't he? Anne, I cherish your innocence, but you don't know the first thing about Italian men. Now, listen, if there's anyone in Rome you want to meet, I'll arrange the introductions, okay? And maybe you'd better let me handle the canceling of your plans with Mario."

His patronizing tone made her furious. "How dare you treat me like a two-year-old, Justin Bradley! You'll arrange . . . you'll handle. . . . Don't you think I can do anything myself? And I'm not going to cancel out on a party that could have important consequences for Dragu Cosmetics, so there!"

"Well, pardon me, Patty Professional!" he yelled back. "Go ahead, make a laughingstock of yourself." He reached for his clothes at the foot of the bed and began to dress with short, jerky movements. Still naked, Anne felt at a disadvantage and pulled back the quilt and got under the covers, drawing the top sheet up to her chin.

"But don't think you can go back and forth between

me and Mario," he warned, slamming into his Italian loafers.

Now fully dressed, Justin stood by the side of the bed and glared down at her. "I'll give you one more chance, Anne, but it's all or nothing. If you go to that party with Mario tomorrow night, don't expect things to be the same between us. I can find plenty of other women to warm my bed, you know."

"Why you—!" Anne cried out in a mixture of hurt and rage. "Is that how you think of me—as a bed warmer? You're the most insufferable, the most arrogant, the most unfeeling—"

"You're the one who's unfeeling, Anne," he cut in quietly. And before she could say anything more, he stalked out of the bedroom.

She winced as the door to the outer room slammed shut with a resounding thud.

- *10* -

AFTER JUSTIN STORMED out of the suite, Anne lay awake for hours replaying their quarrel over and over in her mind. The more she thought about it, the angrier she became. Just who did Justin Bradley think he was, dictating to her, delivering ultimatums, acting no better than a caveman? He had insulted her professional integrity, he had implied that the principessa's party was going to be some sort of decadent bacchanalia, and, worst of all, he had made that parting crack about other women to warm his bed. Well, let them, Anne thought, seizing a pillow and throwing it across the room.

Then she remembered she was still wearing the ankle bracelet he had given her. She reached under the covers and unclasped it, thinking to fling it after the pillow. But her glance rested on the romantic motif, and suddenly her hand was paralyzed. She fought the tears that welled inside her and put the ornament in the drawer of her bedside table.

I won't wear his damned slave bracelet, she thought darkly, yet with the gift out of sight she felt strangely forlorn. She steeled herself against this sensation of vulnerability by again recalling his cutting reference to other women. Her anger returned full force. As far as she was concerned, any woman who wanted Justin Bradley was welcome to him. From now on she would have nothing to do with the man outside of their professional dealings.

And maybe that's what Justin wanted. Maybe now that he'd gotten her into bed—had had her, as he probably phrased it to himself—he had deliberately picked a quarrel with her to avoid any emotional entanglement. Perhaps his declarations of love were all part of his bedroom patter.

But part of her refused to believe he could be so callous. She couldn't accept that the passionate, solicitous man who had transformed the universe for her with his lovemaking could be a total fraud.

In the morning she was awakened from a fitful sleep by the jangling of the telephone. Despite all her dark thoughts the night before, she hoped it was Justin calling to apologize. Well, why not? If he could admit he'd been wrong, if he really did care about her, why shouldn't she forgive him? She would even be magnanimous and offer to leave the party early and come to his hotel. When she finally picked up the receiver, Anne was feeling almost cheerful again.

"Annina, I hope I did not wake you?"

Anne's heart plummeted. "Oh, hello, Mario. Not really. It doesn't matter."

"But of course it matters. I am sorry to disturb you. But I must speak with you as soon as possible. Can you get dressed and come over to the salon right away?"

Anne felt a surge of irritation. Now Mario was starting! Come to me right away, this minute—were all men like that? Trying to keep her voice even, Anne asked, "Mario, can't it wait until tonight? You are escorting me to the principessa's, after all."

There was a long silence. When Mario finally spoke, Anne thought he sounded embarrassed. "Annina, I cannot explain over the phone, but it is important that I see you this morning."

"All right, Mario," she capitulated. "I'll be there in half an hour."

Mario had obviously been on the lookout for her arrival, because he met her at the front of the salon and propelled her quickly out the door to a sidewalk café on the Via Condotti. "We will talk over cappuccino," he said. "But first I must tell you how becoming that quilted silk jacket is on you. I knew royal blue would be perfect with your hair, and it is."

"I'm not sure if that's a compliment to me or you," she teased.

He joined in her laughter. "I was never known for my modesty," he admitted. As usual, he was nattily attired, in an exuberant plaid shirt of various pinks, yellows, and oranges, black corduroy pants, and a matching vest. Anne couldn't imagine any other man in such an ensemble, but he wore it with panache.

When the waiter had brought their cappuccini, Mario cleared his throat, then spread his large hands in a helpless gesture. "Annina, I do not quite know how to begin," he said. "You see, I am in an awkward position. Monica came to my apartment last night and we—we made up. She told me she had thought everything over and would agree to tell her parents of our engagement directly after the showing of my fall collection. She is sure it will be a big success, with lots of publicity, and then there will be the announcement of my collaboration with Dragu. She tells me her family will have more respect for me as a consequence. And even if they do not, she agrees to marry me anyway."

"Oh, but that's wonderful, Mario!" Anne exclaimed, forgetting everything else in her genuine happiness for him.

He smiled ruefully. "Yes, it is wonderful for me. But

you see, Monica expects me to take her to the principessa's soirée. To tell you the truth, I think it was the idea of my appearing tonight before all our friends with another woman that caused her to reconsider our engagement in the first place. However, I do not look the gift horse in the mouth. I am happy, but you, Annina . . ."

The light dawned for Anne. "I see, Mario. You are troubled about letting me down. Well, don't give it another thought. Of course you must go to the principessa's with Monica." Strangely, she felt no disappointment about missing the soirée, but she couldn't help being aware that her blowup with Justin had been for nothing, and the irony was bitter to her. However, she wasn't going to reveal this to Mario and have him feel responsible.

Mario reached across the table and took her hands. "You are too good, Annina," he said, his face radiant. "But tell me, has Signor Bradley returned from Milan? Because if he has, then you will be able to go to the principessa's after all, and with the man you truly care for—that is even better, no?"

Anne covered her confusion by taking a sip of cappuccino. "Justin is back, Mario, but—"

"Then everything is perfect!" he exulted. "The Olivettis will also be going to the principessa's tonight. I have only to call the maestro and I am sure he can get permission to bring you and Signor Bradley as his guests."

Anne shook her head. "That's impossible, Mario. Justin and I have quarreled."

Mario frowned. "Over La Tiziana? But no, I see in your face that is not it. *Dio mìo*—I guess it all. You told Signor Bradley you were going to this party with me and he went into a jealous rage, no? But that is terrible. I must fix everything."

"Please, Mario, I'd rather you left it alone. It's not a question of simple jealousy. Justin hinted at some sort of scandal connected with the party. He didn't want me to go at all."

Mario waved his arm in a dismissive gesture. "He was jealous, I am sure that is the heart of the matter. But it is true that our Roman parties are sometimes a bit wild. There are principessas and principessas, but I assure you that the di Benedetti is the most respectable sort. The mayor is attending this party. There will even be a few cardinals. Maestro Olivetti will remove any doubts from Signor Bradley's mind. Annina, do not look so hopeless. You are perhaps worried that I will tell the maestro all about your personal affairs? But of course not. I have the discretion. I will only make sure that he insists your friend attend the party and bring you with him. You will see, I will take care of everything."

Anne was about to protest, but a thought struck her. If Justin had been sincere in his objections to her attending the soirée because he thought it was going to be an orgy, or if, as Mario seemed to think, he had merely been jealous of her spending an evening with another man, wouldn't Olivetti's intervention set him straight? On the other hand, if he didn't relent, wouldn't that prove he had only been looking for an excuse to discard her now that he had gotten her into bed? She had to know if he had been using her.

"All right, Mario," she said. "If Justin asks me to the soirée, I will accept."

"He will ask. You just leave it to me," Mario promised confidently.

By two o'clock that afternoon Anne had her doubts. Since returning from the café she had been waiting for Justin to telephone, and he hadn't. She had even had room service send up lunch so as not to miss the call that had never come. It was humiliating. Then, at two-thirty, she heard someone knock. Thinking it must be one of the hotel personnel, she went to the door and opened it. Justin!

Though haggard, his aristocratic face was as handsome as ever. There were dark circles beneath his golden-brown eyes, which glinted at her with an indecipherable expression. As usual he was impeccably dressed, in a light-blue three-piece suit with a navy tie. As her eyes took in his long length, the memory of last night's lovemaking rushed over her, and her knees went weak. She was filled with a throbbing need. She longed to rush into his masterful arms, to taste the intoxicating kiss of his sensual mouth, to feel his lean, rugged maleness pressed against her. . . . But pride conquered desire and she merely stood there.

For a moment they remained frozen, staring at each other. Justin was the first to avert his gaze. "I'm sorry to barge up here like this," he said woodenly, raking his hand through his hair, "but I figured if I asked the desk clerk to announce me, you'd have him tell me to go to hell."

When she saw his sheepish expression, Anne's heart softened. Yet somehow she couldn't be the first to let down the barriers they had erected against each other.

"Well, since you're here, you might as well come in and sit down," she told him stiffly. She led him to the low sofa in the outer room of her suite and seated herself in a green armchair across the coffee table from him.

"I've been with Maestro Olivetti all morning," he began awkwardly. "We just had lunch together. I should have a contract ready for you to look at on Monday."

"I'm glad to hear it," she said, "but surely you didn't stop by just to tell me that." After their lovemaking of the previous night, she felt as if she belonged to him irrevocably, and her whole being yearned for his touch. But he owed her an apology, and it didn't seem to be forthcoming.

"You're right. That isn't why I came." There was a long pause, then he said, "The maestro suggested I invite you to the gala at the Principessa di Benedetti's tonight. I gather something's come up for Marini, and you need an escort."

She couldn't bear sitting across from him like this, the few feet separating them seeming like miles. Rising abruptly, she went over to the marble mantelpiece and leaned against it. With her back to him she asked, "Do you want to take me, Justin?"

"To the principessa's? No. But I know how much you want to go and Olivetti assures me it's all on the up and up."

She sighed. "If you really want to know, Justin, I loathe large parties. It's just that I feel a professional obligation to attend. The countess told me on the phone that she plans on sending me abroad more often."

"I didn't know that. I can see why you'd want to meet the movers and shakers of Roman society, then."

She sensed his presence behind her before she felt his hands on her shoulders, turning her toward him. As if of their own accord, their bodies seemed to mold toward each other, and she felt him press tightly against her as his arms went around her waist in an all-encompassing embrace.

"Anne, Anne, Anne," he murmured hoarsely. "My love. You feel so good, you smell so good. Forgive me for all the cutting things I said last night, darling. I was mad with jealousy, furious that you seemed to care more about Mario's feelings than mine, as if what had happened between us meant nothing to you."

"How can you say that?" she asked. "It meant everything to me." She reached up and caressed the supple skin of his cheek.

"You mean everything to me, Anne." Cupping her chin in his hand, he tilted her face toward his. "You seem to bring out the best . . . and the worst . . . in me," he confessed. "I couldn't bear the thought of all those men looking at you, and Mario—"

"Justin, please let's not quarrel again about Mario," she pleaded.

"I don't trust him," Justin said darkly. "But I should have trusted you. Only you sounded so brittle—the good news . . . the bad news . . ."

"I didn't know what to say . . ."

"It wasn't your fault, *carissima*. I acted like a caveman. It's just that I've never felt this way about any woman. I'm so crazy with love for you, I want to be with you every second of the day and night."

"Oh, Justin," she said softly, "I feel the same way about you."

"How I've longed to hear you say that!" he said passionately, engulfing her in an ardent embrace. "From the very first moment I ached for you, but you were so aloof. Last night I was beginning to worry that you just weren't interested in me. And then when we confided in each other I felt so close to you, and I hoped you felt the same way about me. When we made love, you were so responsive . . ."

Justin vulnerable? Justin fearing rejection? It put him in a new and appealing light. "I guess I was trying to keep you at bay," Anne confessed, "but you know that was because of Chuck. You sensed what had happened before I even told you about it."

"I had to think you'd been hurt by another man. The only alternative was to accept that you just weren't interested. I don't think my ego could have taken it—or my heart."

She laughed softly. "Justin, you make it sound as if you'd been pursuing me for ages. Do you realize that the total amount of time we've spent together is well under a week?"

He nibbled at her earlobe. "Bosh, as Marie would say. Quality, not quantity. Besides, if we were seeing each other in New York once a week, it would come down to the same number of hours over a longer period. To me, it seems like ages—especially when I think of all the nights I've slept alone since meeting you."

"You don't like sleeping alone?" she teased.

"I don't like sleeping without you. Last night was the worst. I was anticipating the joy of holding you in my arms all night, and then I blew it so completely. I don't think I had an hour's sleep for wondering if you'd ever speak to me again about anything other than our business here."

"Why didn't you call?" She shivered slightly as his fingers traced a path over her ears and cheeks, and down to her cleavage.

"Last night I figured you'd hang up," he admitted, "and then this morning I was under the eagle eye of Olivetti. I thought about ducking into a phone booth at lunch, but I knew I had to see you. I was all primed to tell you how sorry I was as soon as you opened the door, but then I got paralyzed by the hostile atmosphere and somehow ended up apologizing for coming up here unannounced instead."

"The atmosphere isn't hostile anymore," she murmured, raising her face in invitation.

The kiss that followed was the longest and sweetest Anne had ever known. An incandescent flame ignited within her at the touch of Justin's velvety lips on hers, and when his tongue entered her mouth, a gentle plunderer that bestowed as much nectar as it took away, the flame became a raging bonfire. His strong arms clasped her to him so firmly that she felt as if she were held in a vise of steel. But she had no desire to escape. Her whole being longed for the total union they had achieved last night, and when at last the kiss ended, their eyes met in a look of intense yearning.

He shook his head reluctantly. "If I don't leave now," he said huskily, "I have a feeling we'll never make it to the principessa's. We're invited to the Olivettis' for drinks first. I'll pick you up at seven. All right?"

"All right," she said. The hours until she would see him again seemed to stretch before her interminably.

"I love you, Anne."

"I love you, Justin."

He kissed her forehead lightly. "I'll see you at seven, then. And I'm looking forward to it."

"Looking forward to the principessa's?" she asked.

"Of course not. To afterward," he said with a rakish chuckle.

- *11* -

THE GOWN MARIO had given Anne for the principessa's soirée was an exquisite creation of frothy black lace belted in a cerulean satin that highlighted the unique light blue of her eyes and made them seem even larger and more incandescent than usual. The dress was strapless, with a stiff flounce of lace at the top of the low-cut bodice, and a full, tiered skirt that reminded Anne of something out of old Seville. Her only worry had been that she had no jewelry elegant enough to wear with the gown, but Mario had dismissed this reservation with a wave of his hand.

"The dress does not call for jewelry," he said. "There is the bow at the waist for ornamentation, and the long gloves of matching black lace for your arms."

"But my shoulders . . . all that bare skin," Anne said dubiously.

"The skin is flawless, and the shoulders are magnificent," Mario assured her. "And your wonderful hair, like flowing copper, will provide all the interest needed at the neck and face."

Now, as she brushed out her shimmering mane, Anne realized, too, that with her hair gracing her shoulders she felt less exposed. And as it turned out, she did have one piece of jewelry to wear, the delicate ankle bracelet that was the token of Justin's love. With a brimming heart she took it from the drawer of her bedside table and fastened it onto her right leg. She would never remove if again!

All that remained was her makeup. Fortunately, she had a panoply of cosmetics from which to choose. She selected a silvery blue eye shadow that the countess had told her had been inspired by her own eyes, a dark brown mascara and eyeliner that matched the natural color of her brows, a deep rose lipstick and a dab of rose blusher on each of her high cheekbones. Sheer black stockings and black satin evening slippers, with a small evening bag made from the same fabric as the belt of her dress, completed Anne's ensemble.

Justin, looking like an advertisement from *Gentleman's Quarterly* in black tails and white tie, expressed his approval of her appearance with characteristic innuendo. "I can hardly wait to undress you," he said with a mischievous glint in his eyes. "There's something about ripping layer after layer of black lace off a beautiful body that drives me wild with desire."

"And then what do I wear to the next party?" she teased.

"No more parties, that's the idea. Except for the private ones, and just you will do just fine for those."

"Hmmm. So tell me, pirate, do you think I will derive equal titillation from popping all the buttons off your shirt?" she asked archly.

"Absolutely. And I hope that what you find underneath will give you even greater pleasure."

"You're telling me, big boy?" she said in her most seductive Mae West manner.

"Hey, not bad. Not bad at all," he said "Come, *carissima,* your coach is waiting."

"My coach?" She followed him through the hotel's double doors and gasped as Justin led her to a gleaming red Ferrari convertible. He opened the door on the passenger side for her.

"And the beautiful part," he said "is that it won't turn into a pumpkin, at least not until I take it back to the car-rental agency Monday morning. I thought tomorrow we'd take a drive with the top down, maybe go out to the Tivoli gardens for a picnic lunch."

"Sounds like fun," she replied, "but, Justin, when did you get it?"

"This afternoon, of course. That was one of the reasons I was able to tear myself from your arms. It occurred to me that it would be better not to drive to the principessa's with the Olivettis, so that we can leave whenever we want to. You haven't seen Olivetti yet, but I should perhaps warn you that he looks as if he needs ten servants to get him out of a chair—if he can find one large enough to hold him in the first place."

This description of Mario's attorney proved less of an exaggeration than Anne had assumed. When the maestro waddled forth to greet them in the living room of his luxurious apartment near the Piazza Venezia, her first thought was of the mountain that wouldn't come to Mohammed. Then she took in his attire, and a new image came to mind—a picture she had once seen of Benjamin Franklin being presented to the king of France. Although she knew his black knee breeches and long black formal coat had to have been made to order for his enormous girth, they seemed to have come straight from the eighteenth century, as did the black silk hose encasing his stubby legs and the black patent-leather slippers on his surprisingly tiny feet. Above a wing collar and formal white bow tie Anne saw a series of chins, uncountable. And his face, wreathed in smiles, was so amply padded that his eyes looked like two merry black raisins stuck into a plum pudding. Yet the maestro carried his monstrous bulk with a certain stately dignity, and the bejeweled papal order that bounced against his heavy chest, suspended from a gold chain, added to the aura that said this was a personage, not a grotesque.

Signora Olivetti, who had opened the door to them, was herself a large woman, though next to her husband she appeared almost diminutive. Like the maestro she seemed to be in her early sixties, and her hair, again like his, was iron gray, although she had a good deal more of it. It had been styled in a full, pompadour hairdo. Her gown, a royal-purple, gold-threaded silk brocade, had a high round collar topped with a choker of the largest diamonds and amethysts Anne had ever seen except in pictures. Clusters of the same jewels sparkled in her drop earrings.

After Justin and the maestro had performed the introductions and the two couples were seated—Justin and Anne on a silver-upholstered sofa, the maestro in a huge mahogany chair that seemed more like a throne, and Signora Olivetti in a more modest chair of the same design as her husband's—they sipped champagne and listened to a dissertation on the Roman aristocracy delivered by Olivetti.

"The di Benedettis, like many of our best Italian families, are actually part American," he explained. "At the turn of the century the wives of your rich robber barons outdid themselves in their efforts to marry off their daughters to impoverished European nobles. Our penniless Italian aristocracy was only too happy to oblige."

"I never realized that," Anne commented, "although now I understand why the principessa speaks English so fluently."

"Ah, but we Italians are natural linguists," the mammoth attorney told her. "My American friends are constantly complaining to me that they come over here to practice their Berlitz Italian and find that everyone from hotel personnel to street vendors insists on addressing them in the latest American slang."

Their conversation shifted then to Rome, and the myriad treasures that Anne must absolutely not leave without seeing. Realizing that she would not have time to take in even a third of them, she began to feel despondent, but Justin broke into the Olivettis' catalog to tell them that he had personally escorted Anne to the Trevi Fountain and thus ensured that she would return to Rome to make up for what she missed the first time.

"And of course you still won't have seen it all," he told her, "so you'll just have to throw another coin in the fountain before you leave."

"Speaking of leaving," Signora Olivetti said gracefully, "I'm afraid we'd better be off for the evening ourselves. Though it is fashionable to be late, the maestro and I would like to introduce you to a few people you should know before the crush at the di Benedettis' gets so great we can't find anyone."

The Palazzo di Benedetti, situated in the shadow of the Palazzo Farnese, nearly rivaled the more famous palace in splendor. Even the proportions of the windows set into the imposing travertine structure and the details of the cornice bespoke the grandeur of a bygone era. Walking through the palace's massive doors on Justin's arm, Anne saw lines of footmen in scarlet velvet knee breeches, long coats trimmed in gold braid, and powdered wigs. The footmen held aloft flaming torches, which lit the way through a cobbled courtyard where a fountain spurted out of a lichen-covered niche beneath the arches of a noble loggia. They mounted a grand marble staircase to a balustrade where gods, nymphs, and satyrs seemed to frolic and cavort in marble-bound merriment. Following the Olivettis through a series of ornate salons lit by hundreds of candles, Anne and Justin at last entered a ballroom of such regal proportions that it reduced the other rooms, wrapped in their green or red or blue silk brocade, to the status of antechambers.

It was a storybook ballroom, from the gleaming parquet floor to the white-and-gold-trimmed ceiling, the dome of which was frescoed with some baroque painter's concept of a sunny day in heaven. The walls were ringed with green malachite columns, and one wall was paneled completely with mirrors. On a dais in one corner of the magnificent room a small string orchestra was playing a composition by Vivaldi.

In the glow of candlelit crystal chandeliers and innumerable bronze torches exquisitely gowned and jeweled women wandered to and fro, escorted by formally attired men. Many of the latter wore diagonally draped red ceremonial sashes punctuated by glittering badges. Across the black lapels of others, rows of miniature medals added color and cachet to the occasion. The fashionable throng laughed and talked or smoked and chattered or greeted one another with glad cries of delight, while still more liveried and bewigged footmen approached them with trays of tiny, beautifully wrought hors d'oeuvres and crystal glasses filled with champagne.

Amid the bustle Anne spotted the Principessa di Benedetti sweeping toward them, her emaciated form resplendent in a voluminous white peau de soie evening gown with a collar of emeralds and a matching emerald tiara in her jet black hair.

"Maestro, Clara, so glad you could make it," she greeted the Olivettis warmly. Then she turned to Anne and Justin. "Ah, it is Mario's great friend, Signorina Hopkins. And this must be your colleague, Signor Bradley. *Piacere.*" Her sharp eyes lingered on Justin approvingly. "Come," she continued, "I will introduce you to my husband. He is over at the bar with my brother-in-law."

"We're in luck," the maestro murmured to Anne as they followed the principessa across the ballroom. "Her brother-in-law is the minister of commerce."

The minister, a tall, debonair man in his early fifties, seemed more like royalty than the Prìncipe di Benedetti, Anne thought, surprised to discover that the principessa's husband was a roly-poly cherub of a man nearly a head shorter than his wife. As she conversed easily with the two men and their wives, she noticed how often Justin was accosted by people who treated him as an old friend, most of them women. As they chatted with various other guests, a number of women took Anne aside for a moment to whisper how charming they found Signor Bradley, and how they envied Anne the adoration with which he looked at her. Her heart glowed with love and pride.

In the course of the next few hours Anne met the heads of several of Rome's largest department stores, a number of wealthy industrialists and their wives, a film producer, a novelist, assorted marchesi and marchese, prìncipi and principesse, conti and contesse, and the mayor of Rome.

It was nearly eleven o'clock when Mario and Monica made their entrance. The model looked stunning in a form-fitting beaded magenta gown, her hair swept up with tiny diamonds scattered throughout the dark tresses. Mario wore a cummerbund and bow tie of the same shade as Monica's dress with his black tuxedo.

Justin's eyebrows lifted in surprise as he followed Anne's gaze to the doorway and saw the couple. "I thought Mario couldn't make it," he said in a low voice.

In an equally low voice she rapidly explained the circumstances.

"I see. So they're engaged to be engaged, are they?" he commented mildly. "Well, I suppose we'd better go over and say hello. Excuse us," he said to the group of celebrities with whom they'd been chatting. They had lost the Olivettis in the crowd some moments before.

By the time they reached Mario, he was alone. "Annina!" He greeted Anne with an effusive hug. "The black lace suits you to perfection, as I knew it would. And Signor Bradley, it is good to see you again." He nodded to Justin.

Justin returned the nod, rather stiffly, Anne thought. "But what's happened to Monica, Mario?" she asked quickly.

"Her friend Angela has whisked her off to the powder room for a gossip," the designer explained. "And what of the Olivettis? I thought you were accompanying them tonight."

"We did," Justin said, "but we seem to have gotten separated from them."

Mario frowned. "Oh, but that is too bad. I was counting on the maestro to present Annina to *tutta Roma*."

"I've been presented," Anne assured him, ticking off the list of important people she had met.

"Benissimo." Mario beamed. "But there are perhaps a few other people I could introduce you to myself."

Before he could go on, Justin cut in smoothly, "Actually, we were just going out on the balcony to get a breath of air. Anne was feeling a little claustrophobic. We'll find you and Monica later, Signor Marini."

"But of course," Mario agreed politely. "There is a buffet at midnight. Why don't we all get together for that? In the meantime, enjoy yourselves."

As Justin steered her away, Anne asked, "Don't you think you were a little abrupt with him, Justin? And I never said I was feeling claustrophobic."

"Don't worry about Marini," he told her. "I'm sure he can understand that I'd like a few minutes alone with you. As for how you're feeling, I can see in your face that all the smoke and the crush are getting to you."

When they were out on the small balcony, overlooking an awesome panorama of the city aglow with winking lights, Anne had to admit that Justin had a point. "It does feel good to let my arms breathe for a moment," she acknowledged, taking off her gloves and hanging them over the side of the wrought iron railing.

"Finally I have you all to myself," Justin said huskily,

drawing her close. "You're the most desirable woman ever created, and there's not a man in there who doesn't know it." He leaned back and traced the curve of her lips with a seductive finger. "I want you so much, Anne. What do you say we make our *buona seras* and get out of here?"

"Shouldn't we stay for the buffet at least?" she asked dubiously. "Mario's expecting us to eat with him and Monica, remember."

Justin sighed. "Can't you forget about him for a moment? Can't you forget about everything but the night and the stars and me?"

She wasn't sure why he was annoyed, but she was determined not to let anything spoil this weekend. "What night? What stars?" she said softly. "I've got only one thing on my mind, Justin." Before he could respond, she put her arms around him and kissed him, relieved to feel the tension in him melt away as his hands tightened around her back and his tongue seared her mouth as if he were branding her his own forever.

- *12* -

It was close to two a.m. when Anne and Justin entered the palatial lobby of the Grand Hotel, where Justin was staying, and made their way across the marble floor dotted with thick Oriental rugs to the elevator.

"Home at last," he murmured seductively in her ear.

"Some home!" Anne exclaimed, gazing dazedly at the elaborate crystal chandeliers, luxuriant potted palms, exquisite antique clocks and wall sconces, and ornate Louis XVI furnishings that made the partitioned lounges of the lobby a picture of old-world magnificence. "No wonder you took the Palazzo di Benedetti in stride. This place is worthy of the Medicis."

"Try the Borgias or the Cencis," Justin corrected as they stepped into the most luxurious elevator Anne had ever seen. Its walls were covered in burgundy Florentine leather that had been beautifully hand tooled with antique gold fleurs-de-lis. The thick, plush carpet was also a deep burgundy. "The Medicis were in Florence," he explained.

"Whatever," Anne said, taking the hand he offered as they stepped out of the elevator and headed toward Justin's suite. When he unlocked the door and switched on the light, she was even further taken aback. The sitting

139

room was nearly as big as the whole lobby of her hotel. It was carpeted in soft blue, and over the carpet were laid two glorious Chinese rugs. One defined a seating area encompassing a darker blue upholstered sofa and two huge chairs, all attended by their own side tables and converging on an exquisite walnut coffee table. The other rug was laid in front of a carved white marble fireplace. The walls were paneled in a patterned gold silk that matched the drapes at the floor-to-ceiling windows.

"Save your admiration for my satin sheets," Justin teased, leading her into the bedroom. There he flicked on the light in an enormous walk-in closet. "You'd better put that dress of yours in here. But let me do the honors."

"We'll undress each other," she whispered with a playful leer. Amid much laughter and many caresses, they managed to get each other out of their elegant finery and hang it up in the closet. Then Justin led her over the thick carpeting to a huge carved walnut bed.

"The sheets really are satin," Anne said in amazement.

"Never mind the sheets," Justin said, covering her body with his and kissing her deeply. Soon Anne forgot everything but him . . . and the wonderful feelings he was evoking in her.

She awoke the next morning nestled like a spoon against Justin. Gently removing his hand from her breast, she turned to survey his sleeping form. He was devastatingly attractive as he lay there, his wavy hair falling engagingly over his high forehead and his lips curved into a sensuous smile. As she had been longing to do for some time, she traced his dimples lightly with her fingertips.

Justin's smile deepened, and he cocked a lazy eye at her. "Mmm—lower, lower," he crooned. "Or did last night tire you out?"

"Who's tired? I can never get enough of you," she

said seductively, snuggling into his arms.

"Nor I of you," he replied tenderly, drawing her tightly against his sinewy body. As their fingers began loving explorations of each other under the covers, he told her, "You know something, Anne? You have magic fingers."

"You're the magic one," she said as his tantalizing caresses bathed her in a voluptuous glow.

"My own Anne. My loveliest of loves." He stroked lightly up and down her bare legs and tickled the soles of her feet in a feathery motion.

"Justin. *Caro, carissimo* Justin." She ran her hands through the curly mat of his chest, over his flat belly, and down to the wellspring of his desire.

"Don't stop touching me," he moaned, cupping her breasts and massaging the creamy globes with exquisite finesse. Erotically his fingertips circled the dusky areolae, then caressed the hard buds that seemed to blossom at his touch. A low groan escaped her throat as his tongue chased away his hands and he laved the sensitized skin with urgent intimacy.

She rippled her fingers through his hair. "It feels so beautiful when you kiss me there."

"I want to kiss you everywhere," he told her, and his tongue proceeded to blaze a trail of liquid fire in all her most sensitive places.

With answering caresses she tried to convey all the love that she felt could never be fully expressed in words. The total intimacy she shared with him was ineffably precious to her, and a prayer of thanks overflowed in her heart.

At the same instant they turned sideways toward each other, and with a duet of murmured endearments, they became one. The music of their lovemaking encompassed ecstatic arias, poignant pianissimos, and fiery fugues, counterpointed by the lyrical chanting of love words. It culminated in a final crescendo that brought them together on a chord of total fulfillment.

Afterward, as they lay blissfully in each other's arms, Justin asked, "Are you up for an afternoon jaunt, or shall we just continue like this all day?"

"Don't tempt me," she said, laughing. "You know, you really are incredible."

"You are too," he said, giving her a light kiss on the forehead before sitting up. "Shall we take a shower together?" he suggested with a wide grin.

"Maybe," she said, being coy. Suddenly she remembered. "Justin! I have no clothes here except my evening gown!"

"Don't worry. After our shower I'll get dressed and go over to your hotel. Give me your key and tell me what to get, and I'll bring the clothes back to you. I have the Ferrari, remember?"

"That's right," she said. "We're going for a drive today, aren't we?"

As it turned out, however, rain was falling heavily by the time Justin returned from the Raphael with Anne's clothing. He suggested they spend the afternoon sightseeing at the Vatican. "At Saint Peter's we can pray for sunny skies," he said with a grin.

Their prayers were answered. When they emerged from the Vatican museums in the late afternoon, the rain had already stopped. After a night during which Anne marveled once again at Justin's sexual prowess and infinite tenderness, they awoke to a glorious spring day.

Before leaving the city, they stopped at an open market to purchase their picnic fare. Anne had never seen such beautiful produce and flowers. There was a whole section of stalls piled high with fresh fruit, vegetables, and herbs. There were also butcher shops, delicatessens, and dairy and cheese stores built into trucks.

"When the market's over for the day, the vendors simply close up the sides of their trucks and drive off to the next market," Justin explained.

Like the natives, he haggled with force and gusto over

every purchase. "Dickering with Olivetti has honed my bargaining skills," he told Anne, dimpling, as he settled on a price for some oranges and grapes with a produce vendor. From another stand he brought a bag of juicy-looking tomatoes and a stalk of *finocchio*, the licorice-flavored, celerylike vegetable Romans often ate for dessert. At a *salumeria* they purchased prosciutto and salami, and from a cheese shop some soft *bel paese* and a wedge of *percorino*, a salty, piquant cheese made from sheep's milk. Across from the market was a bakery, from which they bought a loaf of oven-warm bread, and a neighboring wine shop sold them a home-filled bottle of a local red wine.

Amply laden with supplies, they got back into the Ferrari and were soon speeding eastward along the cypress-lined Via Tibertina.

"We'll stop for lunch at Hadrian's Villa," Justin told Anne, "and walk around the ruins there. Then we can go out to the Villa d'Este, which has the world's only sculpture garden made of water."

Hadrian's Villa wasn't at all what Anne had anticipated from the name. "Did you say this was a villa or a village?" she quipped as she gazed at the endless green slopes covered with columns, terracings, underground corridors still in the process of excavation, and the remains of what the scale model at the entrance told her had once been theaters, temples, baths, libraries, palaces, and other architectural fantasies.

Justin laughed. "Hadrian was an emperor and a general, and he thought of this as his retirement home. But I'll admit that a hundred and eighty acres makes for one hell of a villa. Still, he had hundreds of friends and hangers-on living with him, not to mention the servants and the guards."

"Plus his wife or mistress. Or maybe mistresses. Yes, mistresses. I'll bet he built the place to house his harem," Anne suggested facetiously.

Justin didn't seem to realize she was teasing. "No, no, this was no pleasure palace. It was meant as a re-creation of some of the wonders of the world that Hadrian had seen on his many travels. He—"

At his earnest tone Anne burst out laughing. Justin gave her a startled look, then began to laugh himself.

"Oh, you were putting me on," he said sheepishly. "Am I boring you with all these historical details?"

"Of course not," she assured him, giving his arm an affectionate squeeze. "I'm impressed to discover that in addition to all your other talents you're an encyclopedia of Roman history as well. I just thought the story called for some romantic interest."

"You and I madly in love with each other—that's all the romantic interest this place needs," Justin said gallantly. He led her through an olive grove to a grassy spot where they sat down on a fallen marble column and set out their picnic on a sun-warmed stone.

"I can see you and Carol are going to hit it off right away," he said, taking off the charcoal-gray blazer that matched his slacks and draping it over a nearby stump of stone. The noon sun shone brilliantly, and Anne was glad she had worn a sleeveless blouse of pale-green chiffon with cool white linen slacks.

"Carol—she's one of your older sisters, isn't she?" Anne recalled.

"Uh huh. She's just two years older than I am, but she loves to tease me when I get off on one of my hobby-horses, like history or opera. She's always saying it's time I got serious about someone and then maybe I wouldn't take myself so seriously. Of course, it's just sibling banter. But I know she'll be delighted with you—although she'll say I don't deserve you," he added, grinning.

Anne felt a glow of pleasure. He wanted to introduce her to this sister, whom he was obviously fond of. "Is Carol married?" she asked.

"Both my sisters are. I'm an uncle many times over. Betsy and her husband live in Alaska now, so I don't see them and their kids all that often. But Carol and Jeff are right in Manhattan, and I visit them fairly frequently when I'm in town. I'm even godfather to their youngest child." He poured the wine into plastic glasses as Anne improvised hero sandwiches.

"Godfather!" She exclaimed. She hadn't guessed that children played a role in Justin's busy life.

"Is that so strange?" he asked her, reaching for a sandwich and handing her a glass of wine. "Cindy and I are actually quite close. She even wants to be an international lawyer when she grows up."

"I'll bet she adores you," Anne guessed. "How old is she?"

"Just twelve, but already a little woman. A few months before her last birthday she said to me, 'Uncle Justin, this year you mustn't buy me a doll for my birthday. I'm too grown up for that now. I'd rather you took me out to dinner at Windows on the World.'"

"And did you?"

"I certainly did. We even had a cocktail before dinner—a Shirley Temple for Cindy, of course," he added hastily. "The captain and our waiter made a big fuss over her, treated her like some glamorous VIP. She had the time of her life."

"Sounds to me like Uncle Justin did some groundwork," Anne teased.

"Oh, I said a word to the maître d' on the phone when I made the reservation," he admitted diffidently. "But Cindy's quite a charmer in her own right." He sighed. "Part of me hates to see her grow up, though. I miss the little imp who used to sit on my knee and demand 'just one more story' before she'd go to bed. I used to invent outrageous adventures about a little girl named Ydnic— that's Cindy backwards. And when she got a little older, we used to talk to each other in pig Latin and op talk—

she was thrilled to think that these 'languages' had been around even in the Dark Ages, when Uncle Justin was a kid." His boyishly disarming smile stretched from ear to ear at the memory.

Anne was forming appealing images of "Uncle Justin"—cuddling little Cindy, entering into her childish world, and loving every minute of it. No wonder he could be so tender, so protective sometimes. "And Cindy's brothers and sisters?" she asked.

"Marc and Michael, the twins, are a few years older than Cindy, and Sharon is a year older than the twins. Cindy's always been my special favorite, but they're all great kids. Maybe one reason I never felt the need to settle down was that Jeff and Carol offered me a ready-made family to be a part of," he mused.

Anne made no reply, still engrossed in the refreshing image of a domesticated Justin playing Peter Pan to Cindy's Wendy.

They munched on their picnic fare in cozy silence, smiling at each other occasionally and laughing conspiratorially when a tour guide passed them recounting the history of the villa to a group of American tourists in very broken English.

"Perhaps you should offer the Italian Tourist Bureau your services," Anne teased. "If you hadn't gone into law, I'm sure you'd have made an excellent *cicerone*."

"I'll have to remember that for my next life," Justin kidded back. "But only if you promise to be reincarnated as one of the tourists I guide."

"I promise," Anne said with a mock-solemnity that made them both laugh again.

"It's true what the man was saying, though," Justin told her. "Hadrian did die just three years after the villa's completion. It seems a shame he didn't get to enjoy it very long after all the work he put into constructing it." He regarded her seriously. "Maybe sometimes it's best not to have everything you could ever want."

"Answered prayers," Anne agreed. At his quizzical look, she explained, "An old saying my mother's fond of: 'Beware of answered prayers.'"

"I see." For a moment he toyed with his wineglass without speaking. "In a way you fall into that category, Anne," he said slowly. "You're like an answered prayer."

"And you don't quite trust that it's all true?" she suggested softly. "I understand, Justin. It's like that for me, too."

"Is it?" His golden-brown eyes gazed at her searchingly. "I told you before how possessive I am, but I never dreamed I could feel the way I do about you. Yesterday, when we were taking a nap at the hotel before dinner and you got up to write postcards to your friends, I found myself jealous. Why is she doing that now, I wondered. Why can't she just be with me?"

"I thought you were asleep," Anne said, surprised. "But even so, Justin, what's half an hour out of an entire weekend?"

"I know my resentment was unreasonable. That's what I mean. I guess what I'm trying to lead up to is—well, I don't want this thing between us to be just some Roman holiday. I love you so much. I want to be with you always."

Anne's heart seemed to stop. Was he going to ask her to marry him? Was that why he had talked about having her meet his favorite sister and told her about his niece? The thought of Justin wanting to marry her filled her with a delicious euphoria. Her every nerve ending tingled with suspense, and her head felt wondrously light she waited mutely for him to continue.

"The idea that when we return to New York you'll be living in the apartment you shared with Chuck bothers me, Anne. Please say you'll move in with me. My place is huge—and without you it will seem very lonely."

His words pierced her like a knife wound. What a romantic fool she'd been! Justin would think her expectations of a marriage proposal preposterous. He knew she'd lived with Chuck, but she hadn't told him that for her it had been a prelude to a lasting commitment. Living together was probably as much of a commitment as this international playboy would ever make.

She struggled to compose herself, to tamp down the bitter feelings of anger and shock that rose to her throat. With feigned calm she reached for a stick of *finocchio*.

"I can't do that, Justin," she said very quietly. "I love you and I want to go on seeing you when we return to New York, but I—I need my own space." A deep wellspring of hurt seemed to bubble up inside her.

"Your space? An apartment you shared with another guy? There are no ghosts at my place, Anne. I've never asked another woman to live with me."

Except Clarissa Stevens, whom you asked to be your wife! her heart screamed. Aloud she said only, "I'm sorry, Justin. Please, can we just table this discussion?"

"If you say so." He began putting away the picnic things. "I guess I brought it up prematurely, Anne, so don't give me your final answer today. Take some time to think about it."

"Sure, I'll do that," she said, knowing she would never change her mind about living with him but not wanting to antagonize him. "And now, how about walking off some of these calories?" she suggested, struggling to keep her tone light.

In a subdued mood they visited the Maritime Theater, a small circular-columned island in the middle of a quiet reflecting pool, and the Canopus, a replica of a sacred canal that linked the Nile to the Temple of Serapis. Justin once again assumed his role of tour guide, and Anne followed him silently through what remained of Hadrian's attempt to construct a heaven on earth. Then, in mutual silence, they drove out to the Villa d'Este. There Anne momentarily lost herself in wonderment at the innumerable fountains of every conceivable size and shape that lined the pathways and flanked the staircases leading up to the princely Renaissance palace, which, Justin informed her, had been in turn a Benedictine convent, a government building, and the private residence of a sixteenth century cardinal and his descendants.

In the car going back to Rome, Justin was the first to speak. "Look, Anne, okay, so you don't want to live with me. But do you have to sulk about it?"

"I'm not sulking," she said defensively. "I have a big day ahead of me tomorrow, and I was thinking about it."

He gave her a quick glance out of the corner of his eyes. "So tell me about your big day," he said.

"Well, in the morning you're bringing over the contracts from Olivetti, and I'll have to go over them," she said. "Then I'm having lunch with some marketing people at Dragu Roma. In the afternoon I suppose you and I should get together and talk about any questions that come up for me about the contracts, and then at night I'm meeting Mario about the cosmetics line."

"Why don't you get together with Mario in the afternoon, and then we can have the evening free and clear," he suggested.

"Mario's not available till nine," she explained. "He expects the salon to be a madhouse, what with the showing on Thursday, so he suggested we get together after working hours. It might be a good idea if you asked Monica out for dinner. I told you last night that the countess wants you to work on her about using Dragu products for the show."

"Why don't we make it a foursome?" Justin suggested. "I'm curious to hear what Marini's got in mind for the new line anyway."

"I don't think that would be appropriate, Justin," she said. "Cosmetics is my beat, remember? Besides, we're not going out. Mario said he'd be pretty tired, so I should just come talk about it over pizza at his apartment."

"His apartment!" Justin's hands clenched the steering wheel so tightly that his knuckles turned white. After a moment's pause he said, "I'm going to pull up at the rest area ahead, Anne. I think we'd better talk about this."

With utmost ease he maneuvered the Ferrari into the left lane and off the road. In one swift movement he turned off the ignition and faced her, raking his fingers through his hair.

"Now, what's all this about going to Marini's apartment?" he demanded.

Part of Anne was gratified by his jealousy, while at the same time she was offended by his innuendo. "Just what are you insinuating, Justin?"

His eyes bored into hers with catlike ferocity. "Don't play games with me. What would you think if one of Dragu's New York buyers suggested a business conference at his apartment?"

She flushed. "The situations are hardly parallel. This is an exceptionally busy time for Mario. He—"

"He's really taken you in, hasn't he? Don't kid yourself that Mario's interest in you is strictly professional, Anne—or should I say Annina? I nearly flipped when I heard that Friday night. Just when did you two get so intimate?"

Anne looked at him levelly. "Mario and I have become friends," she said frostily. "So what? Our friendship isn't 'intimate' in the sense you mean. Have you forgotten that he's just become reengaged to Monica?"

"Big deal. All the more reason for a final fling. Besides, they're not reengaged until after his fall collection is a proven success—if it is a success."

"You just don't like Mario, Justin. That's your problem, not mine."

"Oh, really?" he said acidly. "And whose problem is it if he makes a pass at you tomorrow night? I can see it all now—the negotiations in ruins, Marini accusing you of being a tease, my having to cover for you with Marie—"

"Cut it out!" Anne yelled. "First of all, Mario isn't going to make a pass at me—except in your twisted imagination. Second, even if he did, has it ever occurred to you that I can handle that type of situation?"

She thought of telling him about Paolo, but decided against it. Justin would only crow about having foreseen the marketing manager's attentions and use that as further ammunition against her.

"Furthermore"—her voice dripped icicles—"what is all this patronizing nonsense about covering for me with the countess? I report directly to her, Justin, not to you. If I make any mistakes, I'll take responsibility for them."

"Well, prepare to take responsibility for a real whopper," he gibed. "Your big blue eyes won't get you out of this one."

"Oh!" she sputtered. "That's the limit. You don't take me seriously as a professional at all, do you? You're incapable of seeing women as anything but sex objects. Bed warmers, I believe you put it."

His eyes narrowed and shot golden sparks at her. "That's a hell of a thing to say after I've asked you to live with me. You're the one who's clinging to your precious independence."

"Oh, so that's what this is all about! You can't believe I turned down your magnanimous proposition," she said, her voice heavy with sarcasm, "and now you're getting revenge for the blow to your ego. What about your independence, Justin? If I lived with you, you'd still be jetting all over the globe, and how would I know whom you were spending *your* nights with? And don't tell me to trust you, because it's clear you don't trust me. I don't believe you really love me, Justin. I don't think you know what love is. You just want to have me at your beck and call like all the other women you've been with."

"You have a pretty low opinion of me, don't you?" he said quietly when she'd finished her tirade. His smoldering eyes looked into hers with an unfathomable expression.

"I don't know what to think anymore," she mumbled, averting her eyes from his penetrating gaze and burying her head in the soft leather of the car seat. She felt drained and exhausted and utterly forlorn.

He reached over and tilted her head up to his. Her chin quivered in his hand like a bird as his lips brushed hers softly. Then he began to kiss her in earnest, his searing tongue sending a bolt of lightning to her core. She hated her body for betraying her this way, hated Justin for manipulating her. As his lips began a hot, moist journey down the sensitive skin of her neck, she steeled herself against the pinpricks of desire that electrified her flesh and broke away from him.

"Sex isn't the answer to everything, Justin," she said stiffly.

"Anne—" he began cajolingly.

"We've said enough to each other already, Justin. I'm very confused and upset right now. I need some time by myself to think things out."

"You don't want to come back to the hotel with me?"

"I think it would be better if you dropped me at the Raphael."

"You left some clothes at my place."

"You can bring them over tomorrow with the contracts."

"Are you saying it's over, Anne?"

"No, I'm just saying I need some time apart. We'll talk again Tuesday morning, after I've met with Mario."

"Maybe that's a good idea," he said thoughtfully. "I know I'm right about him, Anne."

"We'll soon see," she replied.

It was the last thing either of them said until they returned to Rome and Justin let her off at the Hotel Raphael.

- *13* -

WHEN JUSTIN CAME to Anne's suite with the contracts and her clothes the next morning, there was still a coolness between them.

"I'd like to read Marie the main clause of the agreement as soon as possible, so please call before four if there's anything you care to discuss," he told her formally.

"I'll do that," she said, equally formally. "I'm sure everything's in apple-pie order," she added more graciously.

"I should hope so," he said shortly. "Cosmetics may be your beat, but contracts are mine. I just thought you might have a problem with some of the legal language."

Anne felt her temper flare. "Do you suppose I've never seen a contract before?" she asked. "Just what do you think a marketing executive does all day?"

"I don't know about all day, but it would appear that she spends her nights conducting business at men's apartments," he returned sardonically.

"Thank you, Walter Wit," Anne countered. "And now, if you'll leave me to my reading—I have a long lunch at noon, if you remember."

"Oh, yes, the Dragu Roma honchos," he said. "That's fine. If you can get back to me right away, I would appreciate it."

It was difficult for Anne to concentrate on percentages, quotas, quality controls, merchandising guarantees, and distribution arrangements after that exchange, but she forced herself to do so. As she had anticipated, all the provisions of the agreement represented an acceptable compromise in both parties' interests, and there were no gaps or ambiguities that might lead to future acrimony.

The only surprise was that Olivetti hadn't held out for a greater share of the profits. His main concern seemed to be getting ironclad assurances that nothing would go out under Mario's name that hadn't been approved at every stage of production by the designer himself. Therefore he stipulated that the products be manufactured in and shipped from Italy alone.

Anne was sure her employer would agree to these provisions. The countess herself had once ordered over a hundred thousand dollars' worth of eye shadow thrown out because the shade of green was infinitesimally darker than the original conception. Anne had not been able to see the difference, but the countess had been adamant.

"If it has my name on it, it has to be exactly as I envisaged it," she roared. "I will not pass off any factory mistakes as mine."

Apparently Mario felt the same way. Fortunately it was cheaper these days to manufacture in Europe anyway, so Anne knew the countess would have no objection to that.

She scanned the contracts quickly a second time, and then, knowing Justin would not yet have returned to his hotel, she called and left a message that she had no questions and he should proceed as discussed. She didn't want to talk to him again until after her meeting with Mario, when she would be able to prove to him how groundless his suspicions had been.

But what if they weren't groundless? Doubt had been nagging at her ever since she had returned to her suite at the Raphael the previous evening. One part of her argued that the idea of Mario trying to seduce her was ludicrous. Still, as Justin had pointed out, one didn't usually conduct business meetings in private apartments.

The problem was that she was now so keyed up, it would be difficult to act naturally with Mario all evening, and that might do as much damage as an actual contretemps. Tossing her gleaming hair over her shoulders, she determined that she would act the same toward Mario this evening as she would have if Justin had never made her apprehensive about the meeting.

But she *was* apprehensive, Anne admitted to herself many hours later as she rang the doorbell of the designer's apartment.

It didn't help to see Mario attired in his customarily tight pants and brilliant-blue silk shirt open almost to his navel. Was this just typical Marini flamboyance, or was he setting a mood, she wondered.

"Annina, come in, come in," he greeted her.

"Good evening, Mario." Her voice sounded natural to her own ears, and with a bravado she didn't feel she returned his hug and stepped purposefully across the threshold into the living room. A ribbon of sheet glass ran around three of the otherwise plain white walls. Through the glass all of Rome lay at their feet. Major monuments were floodlighted and shone like jewels against the midnight velvet of the evening. In counterpoint to the ancient magnificence outside, the living room was furnished in low modern pieces upholstered variously in soft leather or heavy wool tweed. The only color was ivory, but this was set off by a profusion of brightly colored patchwork pillows, obviously made from remnants of fabric from Mario's studio.

"First, Annina, you must tell me what is wrong," the

designer told her authoritatively as he ushered her into the living room and seated himself in a leather upholstered armchair across from the sofa, where he motioned for her to make herself comfortable.

"Wrong?" she said, wondering how she had betrayed herself. "What makes you think anything is wrong, Mario?"

"Annina, I am a designer. When a woman shows up at my apartment on a warm night attired in a long sleeved suit with a scarf that has no business being there tucked into a neckline that is not so low-cut to begin with, and boots covering her legs, no less, I know that something is wrong. Now, tell me why you have wrapped yourself up like a mummy for our conference."

Anne didn't know what to say. "I thought it might turn cool by the time I left," she offered lamely.

"Nonsense! You thought perhaps this meeting was not on the up-and-up because we are at my apartment. But then why didn't you insist on going out in the first place?"

"Oh, Mario, it's not that *I* thought—"

"No?" he interrupted her. "Ah, then it is what Signor Bradley thought. But of course, he is a jealous man, that one."

"I don't know, Mario," Anne said, feeling more relaxed now that the situation was out in the open. "I've given Justin no reason to be jealous."

"Reason?" Mario shrugged. "If human beings were reasonable, it would be a different world, Annina. When a man is jealous, he is jealous. I should know, I am a jealous man myself. Men are like that." He spread his hands in a typical Italian gesture.

"I feel very silly," Anne confessed.

"So take off your jacket and that scarf and you will feel less silly," Mario suggested. "The boots can go, too. You may tuck your feet under yourself if that will make you more comfortable. And I will button a few of my buttons, so you know I have only cosmetics on my mind."

He gave her an elfin grin. "I tell you frankly, Annina, the week before my show I have barely enough energy for Monica, *capisci*? Now let us get down to business. The pizza is in the oven, it will be ready in a few minutes." From a low coffee table he picked up an artist's notebook and began to flip through the pages. Anne saw that they were covered with notes and sketches.

"First, tell me what you think of this idea for the nail polish," Mario began. "From what you said in your report, it is clear that we must come out with something that has never been done before. A different shade of pink or red or orange will not do. Earth tones have been done. Frosted and glittery nail polish have been done. But marbled nail lacquers, that has never been done."

"Marbled?" Anne asked, intrigued.

"Marbled," Mario repeated. "Now, the contessa has already created an Italian mystique for her products. I am an Italian, and naturally my line must be a new variation on that theme. So I thought about it. What is Italy famous for? Among other things, marble. There is the *giallo antico,* which shimmers between a warm yellow and sunset pink. There is *pavonazzetto,* named for the peacock and streaked with many shades of red or violet or purple. There is *africano,* red-on-black. There is already scarlet nail polish, and black nail polish, but where are the two combined?

"You see, we get away from solid colors. We have veins and streaks and mottling, and then the lipstick and the eye shadow and the mascara and the blusher pick up the colors of the marbling."

"Mario, it's brilliant!" Anne exclaimed. "You're right, marbled nail polish is absolutely original, and it allows for so many possibilites in creating a total look."

"Exactly. With the clothes, as well as the makeup. Only Mario Marini could have thought of it," he added immodestly. "Here, why don't you just look at these sketches while I get the pizza. You will have some Chianti, too? I did not want to offer wine when you were troubled by Signor Bradley's suspicions. But it is really not civilized to eat without it."

"I'd love some Chianti," Anne told him heartily.

The lasagna pizza entirely fulfilled Anne's expectations. A thin crust was topped with layers of homemade pasta, filled with ricotta, parmesan, and mozzarella cheeses, and covered with a pungent tomato-meat sauce.

"It is scrumptious, no?" Mario asked. "I am so glad you taught me that word. It gave me a wonderful idea for the perfume line."

Anne looked at him questioningly. "Surely not lasagna perfume?"

He threw back his head and laughed. "No, no, no. Let me explain the analogy. As you are eating the pizza, how do you feel?"

Anne reflected. "Like I can't wait to eat it all up, it's so delicious," she said.

"*Giusto*. And that is what a perfume should do for a woman—make her smell so delicious that the man wants to eat her all up. You even have a saying, no? 'The way to a man's heart is through his stomach.'"

"That's true," Anne said. "And we also speak of a sexy woman as a piece of cheesecake or a cream puff."

"You see? Now, there are many different ingredients that go into a perfume," Mario said, "but there is an overall scent, a certain definitive flavor. For this we will use the most appetizing aromas—cinnamon, vanilla, anise. No floral scents—who wants to eat a bouquet of flowers? Some fruity scents perhaps, but not apple or orange; that, too, has been overdone. Persimmon, kiwi, mango, papaya—we will stick to the exotic fruits. Perhaps we will even combine the fruits and spices."

"It would lend itself well to picture ads and commercials," Anne said slowly. "You know, the idea that the man is hungering after the woman, burying his head in her neck and that sort of thing. What did you have in mind for the bottles?"

"Ah, yes, the bottles." Mario flipped through his notebook to a page of sketches. "The bottles will themselves be works of art. You have heard of Murano glass? It is exquisite, hand blown, every color of the rainbow. When the woman has used up all the perfume, she will save the container as an *objet d'art*."

Anne took a sip of wine. "Mario, you're a genius," she breathed.

"Naturally," he agreed, his eyes twinkling. "That is why you came to me in the first place."

It was nearly one o'clock when Anne returned to her hotel in a state of jubilation. She was too excited to sleep and decided she might as well call the countess at home and make her report immediately. Otherwise, she would have to wait until tomorrow afternoon, because of the Rome-New York time difference.

The countess was as enthusiastic about Mario's ideas as Anne was.

"Thank God we got to him before any of our competitors," she said. "I owe that to you, Anne. There's been a lot of talk in the New York fashion world about that fall collection of his, and my sources tell me that some of my rivals have gone to Rome for it already. Justin got that agreement down none too soon. I'm very pleased with it, by the way. What do you think?"

"It's an excellent contract," Anne agreed.

"And you're going to have the signing on Thursday?"

"Yes," Anne said; then a thought struck her. "Maybe we shouldn't wait until the collection has been shown," she said. "I know we thought that would be the ideal moment publicity-wise, but now I'm not so sure. Justin and I went to this party the other night, and everyone was talking about what a triumph Mario's showing is going to be. It's being held in a huge palace, and the whole event is going to be a much bigger deal than I originally thought. We might end up as a footnote. After all, my face isn't exactly known to the world, and the photographers may want to concentrate on shots of Mario and his models. It would be different if you were here, Countess. As your representative, I simply don't have the same clout."

"You will, my dear, you will. I'm going to make you my international liaison, you know. But it's true, at this juncture you might get lost in the shuffle."

"I think at some point you ought to come over yourself for pictures with Mario," Anne suggested. "We can have a whole publicity fanfare then. And if we're not waiting until Thursday to sign the contracts, I don't see why we can't do it now. Mario just might have second thoughts, decide the impetus of his showing entitles him to a bigger piece of the action. Or he might be able to get the financial backing to bring out a totally independent line of cosmetics, and then he wouldn't need us at all."

"Or he might get an offer he just couldn't refuse from Revlon or Elizabeth Arden or Estée Lauder," the countess suggested. "I agree with you. Why take unnecessary risks? I want those contracts signed tomorrow; and I'm going to call Justin right now and tell him so myself. I'll have him call Maestro Olivetti first thing in the morning."

After the countess had hung up Anne prepared for bed. She was awakened from a deep sleep nearly an hour later by the telephone.

"Just what the hell do you think you're doing?" Justin exploded in response to her sleepy hello.

Instantly Anne was wide awake. Checking the luminous dial of her bedside clock, she shot back, "What do you think *you're* doing, Justin, calling at two-thirty in the morning! Checking to see if I'm spending the night with Mario? You couldn't have been more wrong about him, you know."

"You sound disappointed," he jeered, "but never mind about that now. I'm calling at this hour because I just got off the phone with Marie and I'm furious!"

"Because we're signing the contracts a few days early?" she asked. "Why should that make you furious? You're not still afraid the showing's going to be a flop, are you?"

"Don't play Little Miss Innocent with me!" he scoffed. "I don't give a damn when the contracts are signed, but I do mind your calling Marie with this brainstorm of yours without consulting with me first. I have to hear what we're doing from her, for God's sake! I paid you the courtesy of showing you the final agreement before calling our employer about it. But you had the gall to make a major decision on your own and let her communicate it to me."

"Justin, this is all a misunderstanding," Anne told him. "I wasn't trying to go behind your back, or over your head, or whatever it is you think I've done. I only called the countess to tell her about Mario's ideas for the new line, and then we got talking and decided that since his ideas were so terrific—"

"Spare me the praises of Mario," Justin interrupted. "I've just been hearing *ad nauseam* from Marie how wonderful he is and how wonderful you are, too. Well, I don't think you're so wonderful!"

"What *do* you think of me?" she asked shakily.

"You wouldn't want to hear it," he said darkly. "But what do you care? You've got your promotion, Miss Dragu International, and I hope you're satisfied."

Anne was convulsed with anger and hurt. "You have no right to speak to me that way! Your problem Justin, is that you don't know how to deal with women as equals. You're used to dictating all the moves to your lady clients and having them tell you how clever and enterprising you are. You couldn't have been more condescending about showing me that contract, as if I'd have to be a juris doctor to make head or tail of it. I suppose you think I had to sleep my way through my M.B.A. Or do you just feel threatened by a woman with a degree in business?"

"I do not feel threatened by your degree, and I have never implied that you earned it by anything except intelligence and hard work. You're confusing me with that creep you used to live with, taking your anger at him out on me. You've been doing that all along, haven't you? Setting me up for a kick in the teeth because some guy once did it to you."

"Is that what you thought I was doing this weekend?" Anne demanded. "Setting you up?"

"I'm supposed to trust you because you went to bed with me? For all I know you were just so sex-starved that any guy would have served the purpose."

"That's hitting below the belt, Justin."

"What do you think you've done to me?"

"I don't think I've done anything to you! It's all in your imagination. Or your ego."

"Leave my ego out of it. We're not communicating, so there's no point in prolonging this discussion. Obviously our personal relationship is finished, but we're still business associates and we've got to wrap up this Marini deal together. I'll call Olivetti and get this contract signing fixed up, so don't leave your hotel tomorrow until you hear from me. Also, I've set it up with Monica about the makeup, and I want you to go over to Dragu Roma with her and the other models on Wednesday. And Thursday we'll go to the showing together. Need I say that neither Olivetti nor Marini nor anyone else involved in this thing should scent the slightest whiff of bad feelings between us?"

"I understand that, Justin. I'll be waiting for your call in the morning. Good night."

After replacing the receiver, Anne switched on the bedside lamp and sat staring into space. How would she ever get through the next few days? Justin angry at her or jealous was one thing, but Justin hating her, thinking she had deliberately stabbed him in the back professionally, was quite another. Was there any justification for his feelings? she asked herself miserably.

She was too devastated by his blunt pronouncement that their personal relationship was finished to be able to sort out what had happened. She needed to talk to someone who could help her see the situation in perspective. She thought of Jeannie.

It was three-thirty by her bedside clock. Anne calculated quickly—nine-thirty, New York time. "Please be there, Jeannie," she prayed as she took the receiver off the hook and dialed.

Her friend answered on the first ring. "Anne! What a coincidence! I was just lying in bed reading a hot romance, and wondering if anything had been happening between you and Justin Bradley."

Anne groaned. "Things have been happening all right. Have you got time to listen to a long story?"

"Sure," Jean answered cheerfully. "Now, just start at the beginning and tell me everything."

There was a pause after Anne had finished her narrative. Then Jean said, "Look, Anne, you're torturing yourself about assigning blame, but that isn't really the issue. Face it, you want the guy back."

"I'm not sure I do," Anne said. "I mean, if he's jealous, unreasonable, can't handle a successful woman—"

"I don't think it's as bad as all that," Jean broke in. "Jealous he is, but not really so unreasonably. After all, the only other time he was serious about a woman, she rejected him. I know it was a long time ago, and there have been others since, but he wasn't in love with them. By the way, who was the first to say 'I love you'—you or him?"

"He was," Anne told her.

"That's what I thought. And he was the one to apologize for your other fight, too. Rightly so, but still—don't you realize he's probably been very unsure of himself with you, Anne? I'm positive that was what was behind all his sound and fury over your going to Mario's. He wanted you to say something like, 'I won't go if you don't want me to, Justin. You mean much more to me than Mario, my career, anything.'"

"How could I have said that, Jeannie? I can't act like a sap just to please Justin."

"Of course not, but you can show him that you care. You've been letting him do a lot of the work in this relationship, honey. Now it's your turn to take the initiative."

"But there's no relationship left," Anne said dismally. "I told you, he's furious about what he perceives as my cutting him out with Dragonescu."

"No, it's not what you did. It's why he thinks you did it," Jean said. "He doesn't believe you really give a damn about him. Look, honey, if he's yelling and screaming and calling you names, there's still a relationship. The opposite of love is indifference."

"But what do I do?" Anne asked.

"Swallow your pride, call him up tomorrow morning. Tell him you're sorry you didn't consult him before phoning the countess. Then tell him you love him."

"Jeannie, I don't think I can."

"Do you want him back?"

"Yes."

"Then do it. He's not going to make the first move this time, Anne."

"I'll give it a try," she promised.

But when she called Justin at ten-thirty the next morning, he gave her no chance to say anything.

"Look, Anne, I told you *I'd* call *you*. I'm waiting for Olivetti to get back to me, and I don't want to tie up the line. So just sit tight and stop pressuring me."

"But, Justin, I only called to apolo—" Anne broke

off in the middle of the word, realizing she was talking to a dial tone.

At twelve Justin rang her back. "Be at Olivetti's office at three." Again he hung up abruptly.

Anne called him back. "Justin, I'm sorry about last night. I didn't mean to sabotage you with the countess. I—I love you."

There was a long silence. "If you mean that, tell me you'll live with me when we get back to New York."

Anne felt her heart sink. "Justin, I want to see a lot of you in New York, but I can't live with you. I just can't."

"Can't? What's preventing you? You mean you don't want to. You think I'm good for your image as an escort, but you don't want any real commitment. Forget it, Anne. You'll have to find some other entrée to the gossip columns."

Once again, she found herself listening to a dial tone.

- *14* -

A BLAZING MIDDAY SUN, more summery than springlike,
shone down on the Casina Valadier as Anne and Justin
rode up to the French-style palace in a taxi for Mario's
showing.

"Napoleon built this place for his son, the King of
Rome, but the boy died young and never got to occupy
it," Justin said blandly as he helped her out of the cab.
"The casina has been put to various uses over the years,
but now the large rooms and halls are used for conferences and showings. There's also a restaurant."

"How fascinating," Anne said, matching his neutral
tone. She wanted to scream. He'd met her at Maestro
Olivetti's office on Tuesday with a mask of geniality,
and had seemed to mock her in the toast to the new
Marini line he had proposed in the champagne celebration
that had followed the contract signing. But as soon as
Mario apologetically told them he had to get back to his
final preparations for the show, Justin maneuvered their
own exit and hustled her into a cab by herself with only
a cursory, "I'll see you Thursday."

Anne had spent yesterday morning at Dragu Roma
getting Monica and the other models squared away with

their makeup, and at Signora Gemini's urging had stayed for a treatment herself in the afternoon. Not that Justin had tried to get in touch—there were no messages when she got back to her hotel. This morning when he'd met her in the lobby of the Raphael, she had hoped the sight of her in the aquamarine silk dress she'd worn on their first date in Rome would provoke some genuine feeling in him, but all he said was, "Run out of new Marinis, Anne? Too bad. But then, all good things do come to an end." He didn't even seem to notice that she was also wearing the gold ankle bracelet he had given her.

They had ridden in silence to the casina, but now that there were other people arriving to observe and overhear them, Justin was once more putting on his act.

Mario had rented the entire palace for the occasion. The showing was held in the elegant ballroom, which was brightened with anemones, daisies, and other fresh spring flowers. Mario's decorators had placed a runway down the length of the room. On either side of this long gray-carpeted ramp were row after row of closely packed gilt chairs, which gave the spectators a good, if stiff-bottomed, view of the models' parade.

There was an air of excited anticipation among the several hundred people gathered for the event. Anne recognized some of the people she had met at the principessa's, and Justin seemed to recognize still more of the spectators. Anne felt as if they were both marionettes as they nodded and smiled on their way to the front of the room, where Mario had reserved seats for them just behind the television crews and photographers. They settled down to watch the show with everyone else.

There was no announcement or master of ceremonies. A burst of gay Neapolitan music captured the audience's attention, and then a stunning model swept from behind a scarlet silk curtain, turned, and fairly pranced down the runway.

The audience vigorously applauded her outfit, a long-waisted blouson top of cherry wool and angora yoked in an eye-catching paisley corduroy of cadmium, absinthe, and teal with a neatly clipped skirt made from the same corduroy as the yoke. When an offstage voice called off the number of the ensemble, Anne could hear the scratching of buyers' pens all around her. She glanced at Justin out of the corner of her eye, but his chiseled features were impassive as he followed the mannequin's progress back up the runway.

The next model was equally well received. She drew back the flaps of her smart oatmeal cotton-poplin raincoat to reveal a tartan-plaid lining in navy and green that matched the slim leather-and-cotton belted dress underneath. A tall blonde followed in a snug poppy-red cashmere sweater dress with a wispy black lace jabot.

Layered dresses with capelike effects seemed to take the audience's fancy. Pure lines, a paintbox of colors, and striking combinations of fabrics were the hallmarks of Mario's daytime wear. Anne especially admired a three-piece suit in plum and yellow with a grosgrain-trimmed mohair jacket and swirly wool skirt whose chenille floral inset recalled the print of the cotton blouse. But it was Monica who brought the house down in a slick gold military-style leather jacket and matching butter-soft slacks, with a bright turquoise cowl-neck sweater underneath. Mario was clearly putting the fashion world on notice that he was having none of the usual muted fall colors or tailored lines.

The evening-wear collection underscored the theme of bold color and imaginative combination of materials. Tuxedo-styled ensembles in a welter of fabrics and every conceivable color alternated with lavish, alluring gowns and prim yet provocative dinner dresses. Metallic yarns and gold- and bronze-encrusted appliqués abounded, and Monica was again a sensation in a molded silver lamé dress whose revealing décolletage narrowed to a seductive black satin flower at the waist. Anne's particular favorites were a sassy cerise velvet evening dress with a stitched satin hip peplum topped by an enormous pale pink silk-organza bow and a rustling violet taffeta ball gown delineated with ruffles.

On and on they came. It seemed to Anne that the buyers never stopped scribbling. Then suddenly the sprightly music came to an abrupt end, and after a suspense-filled hush, the hidden orchestra languourously intoned the familiar strains of *Lohengrin*. The curtains parted and the waiting crowd was treated to the sight of a traditionally veiled bride. She stood shyly before the curtain, then moved gracefully down the runway as the audience murmured its approval.

The bride wore ivory Venetian lace appliquéd over heavy ivory silk satin. The gown's high neck and princess sleeves were embroidered with tiny seed pearls. Seed pearls also trimmed the sweeping hem.

The train was matching Venetian lace and was carried by two angelic-looking, dark-eyed children, a boy and a girl. Both were darling in black velvet and looked very pleased with themselves.

The bride paused at the end of the runway and slowly lifted her veil. It was Monica, her face radiant and ethereal.

Anne couldn't swallow for the lump in her throat. How she longed to float down the aisle in such a dress to meet a waiting Justin at the altar. For a moment her mind mocked her with a vision of the scene. How far that vision was from reality!

Involuntarily she stole a glance at Justin. Through her misted eyes it seemed he was looking at her with a pensive, concerned expression. Then, to her horror, tears welled in her eyes and rolled onto her cheeks. She turned away quickly, struggling to regain control of her emotions, hoping desperately that Justin hadn't noticed.

But apparently he had. She felt something soft being pressed into her hand, and when she looked down, there

was a man's handkerchief resting in her palm. His so-
licitude threatened to undo her completely, and she
couldn't look at him as she raised the folded square of
material and dried her cheeks. Then, hastily, she slipped
the handkerchief into her purse. She was too embarrassed
to acknowledge her momentary weakness by returning
it.

The lilting melody of "Here Comes the Bride" ac-
companied Monica's return to the scarlet silk curtain at
the head of the runway. She paused dramatically as the
music died away, the children scurried off, and Mario
emerged from behind the curtain to join her. Before the
eyes of the astounded audience, he took a small velvet
box from the pocket of what seemed to Anne a most
ungroomlike orange-and-black jumpsuit and removed a
diamond solitaire ring, which he placed on Monica's
finger in an elaborate pantomime. The orchestra struck
up the resounding chords of Mendelssohn's "Wedding
March" as the audience went truly wild.

Mario and Monica remained framed by the curtain,
the designer holding his fiancée's ringed hand aloft, as
the music again returned to an ebullient Neapolitan dance
tune and the other models paraded down the runway amid
good-natured pandemonium. The Marini fall and winter
collection closed to a standing ovation.

"Shall we join the flood backstage and offer our con-
gratulations?" Justin asked close to Anne's ear amid the
uproar. His warm breath tickled her skin and sent a frisson of regret and longing through her every nerve. Not
trusting herself to speak, she merely nodded and turned
to retrieve her purse from the chair where she had left
it.

Just then she noticed an imposing white-haired figure
in a blue-and-silver brocade dress with matching coat
sailing toward them with the tide of people heading backstage. Anne froze, her hand suspended over her purse.
It was none other than Countess Marie Dragutescu.

- 15 -

ANNE'S FIRST THOUGHT on recognizing her employer was that somehow the countess's presence was part of a retaliation scheme on Justin's part for the injury he imagined she had intended him by her midnight call to New York. Then, as he followed her shocked gaze and they turned toward each other their eyes locked and she realized from the hardening of his expression that he thought she was behind Dragonescu's appearance.

"I had no idea she was here," Anne protested quickly, wondering if he caught her words amid the din. He said nothing but merely stood transfixed, as if waiting for the apparition to join them—or vanish into thin air.

"Well, you needn't gawk at me as if I'd dropped from the clouds, although I suppose I did at that, courtesy of Alitalia," the countess boomed at them when she had reached their seats toward the front of the ballroom. "I meant to surprise you two, but not strike terror into your breasts, for pity's sake."

Justin was the first to recover. "Marie, you're looking splendid."

"Harumph. I'm ashamed not to be wearing a Marini, but I could hardly ask Mario to interrupt his preparations for the show yesterday to design something, could I? No matter, I have a special fitting at the salon tomorrow."

Anne found her voice at last. "Mario is expecting you?"

"Of course, my dear, and I'm pleased to see he can keep a secret. Although actually, Anne, you were the one who gave me the idea of flying over. All that talk about pictures of me and Mario together at the proper moment. Today, of course, is Mario's. His collection has set the entire fashion world on its ear. But we're scheduling a press conference for Saturday, and the Dragu-Marini collaboration will be in all the Sunday papers. Harumph, why are we standing here gabbing? Justin, lead the way backstage. I want to meet the newest international fashion superstar in person."

The countess was adamant about not stealing any of Mario's thunder. They waited patiently at the edge of the backstage throng until the last of the reporters had departed before she gave an imperial nod, and Justin and Anne led her forth to where Mario stood surrounded by a clique of champagne-sipping admirers. Monica was at his side, still wearing the fabulous wedding gown.

Anne performed the introductions, and the cosmetics queen and the crown prince of designers were soon chatting away like old friends. Monica, with a warmth Anne had never seen in her before, presented Anne and the countess to her parents, who had apparently flown in for the occasion.

The Arlettis were obviously impressed by the countess's aristocratic title, and Anne could see their prospective son-in-law rise another notch in their estimation as the countess made it clear that she and Mario were a mutual admiration society. However, Anne thought Monica's mother looked wistfully at Justin as he and Anne joined their family circle and left Mario and the countess to their tête-à-tête. Anne felt rather like an interloper among these old friends of Justin's, despite his occasional efforts to draw her into their conversation. She knew his civility was just a façade. She had seen the glint in his eye when the countess had credited Anne with inspiring her trip to Rome.

"Well, if you won't join us—yes, yes, yes, of course. I understand—I'd better be taking Anne and Justin out to lunch," Anne heard the countess tell Mario finally. She gathered that he had been explaining that he was spending the afternoon *en famille* with the Arlettis. "Until tomorrow, then."

The restaurant at the casina was mobbed, and the countess suggested they go elsewhere. "Justin, you know Rome," she said. "Find us a restaurant that doesn't require reservations."

An hour later they were lunching on *saltimbocca,* thin slices of veal and ham seasoned with sage and sautéed lightly in butter, and *carciofi alla romana,* tender artichokes cooked in white wine and flavored with mint and garlic, in a charming courtyard trattoria near the northern end of the Piazza di Spagna. In the cab Justin had seemed to address her as he told them the restaurant he was taking them to was called Otello alla Concordia. Anne had wondered briefly if he was trying to convey a subtle apology for his irrational jealousy of Mario, but then she decided this was wishful thinking. If anything, the name only signified Justin's penchant for operatically titled eateries.

"Well, you've been letting me rattle on and on about this and that, or is it just that you two don't have anything to say for yourselves?" the countess asked them sharply in the midst of one of her own monologues.

"We've had rather a full week, especially Anne," Justin said quickly.

"Yes, yes, I imagine you have. And I commend you both. The Marini cosmetics line has been launched without a single snag in the proceedings," the old woman replied complacently. "It was one of my happier inspirations, sending you two over here together."

The irony of this was too much for Anne, and she excused herself to go to the ladies' room. When she returned to the table, she was conscious that the countess and Justin were both staring at her.

"I was just commenting how becoming that dress is to you, my dear," the countess informed her. "And do you know what Justin replied? 'I think it's rather that Anne becomes the dress,' he said. That's a pretty compliment, now, isn't it?"

"Justin has a golden tongue," Anne responded, wishing he wouldn't lay it on so thickly. She looked across the table at him, but couldn't decipher his expression.

"Mario's fiancée is quite a stunner," the countess continued, pausing to take a long draft from her wineglass. "I hope they'll be very happy together. I was once in love with a Neapolitan myself," she added unexpectedly.

Anne was intrigued. Justin had remarked that he thought there'd been someone in the countess's past, but he hadn't been able to supply any specifics. Was the countess now going to tell them the story herself? Anne waited with bated breath.

"Franco was a vice-president at the Bank of Naples in New York," Marie Dragutescu reminisced fondly. "If it hadn't been for him, there might never have been a Dragu Cosmetics. I'd been to all the American banks, trying to take out a loan to start my own salon, and they turned me down flat, every one of them. Fools!

"In those days it was easier for the proverbial camel to go through the eye of a needle than for a woman to be taken seriously by a banker. But I was determined, so I began to make the rounds of the foreign banks. And there was Franco, at the Bank of Naples, the first one who didn't laugh me out of his office. Instead of bullying me about collateral and cosigners like the rest of those stuffed shirts, he asked me to tell him my ideas about cosmetics.

"'I'm going to create a face cream as light as meringue,' I told him. 'Yes, you are,' he said, 'and the Banco di Napoli is going to help you do it.' Just like that! I think I would have fallen in love with him out of sheer gratitude, but he was elegant, witty, everything else you could want in a man. The months we had together were the happiest of my life."

She paused to refill her wineglass, and Anne looked across the table at Justin, who was gazing intently at the countess.

"He died. Heart attack," the old woman said abruptly. "Of course he was quite a bit older than I, but still too young to go like that. Never even got to see my face cream. But that was the beginning of my Napoli line. All the Italian names were a memorial to him. Everyone thought I was a hard-bitten businesswoman with no time for romance, but that wasn't it. Dragu Cosmetics was a poor substitute for the children Franco and I would never have, but it was somehow a connection.

"Perhaps I was mistaken not to marry someone else. Perhaps I idealized my memories over the years. But when you've had the real thing, it's hard to—to settle. Not that we didn't have our tiffs. Franco was a hot-blooded Italian, and I'm not all sweetness and light myself. But we loved more than we fought. Yes, we loved."

She sighed, then pulled herself up. "I'm babbling like a sentimental old woman. Well, maybe that's what I am. Or maybe it's just the wine and the romantic finale of that fashion show of Mario's, reminding me of what I had—and what I missed."

"Thank you for sharing it with us, Marie," Justin said simply.

"Bessie's the only one I've told the story to before," the countess went on. "I might not even have told her, but she was the first of my employees to get pregnant, and she thought she had to quit over it. Well, I set her straight. They didn't talk about maternity leaves and day-care centers in those days, but I was one of the first to give working women those options. The Dragu nursery facilities are still among the best in Manhattan. No woman has ever had to leave Dragu because of a conflict between career and marriage or family.

"You keep that in mind, my dear"—she turned benign blue eyes on Anne—"when you meet the man who's worthy of you. Just because you're my international liaison now doesn't mean there can't be some flexibility about travel schedules and such."

Anne was acutely embarrassed. She suspected that the countess had decided she and Justin made an attractive couple and was intimating that she wouldn't stand in their way if they decided to do something about it. If only she knew how she was wasting her breath.

"Would anybody care for coffee?" Justin asked easily. He didn't seem the least discomfited by the countess's latter remarks, and Anne envied him. Perhaps it was just that he didn't think the question of Anne's career and potential marriage were of any concern to him. After all, he wouldn't be seeing any more of her after today. His work in Rome was finished, and there was no reason for him not to go back to New York tomorrow.

But apparently there was.

"You look a bit peaked, Justin," the countess remarked as they sipped their espressos. "And, Anne, you probably would look peaked if it weren't for the magic of my cosmetics. So why don't you two go to Venice and relax for a few days? I'll join you there next week. I ought to pay a visit to this glass factory in Murano Mario has in mind for the perfume bottles, and I'll want you two to come with me."

"That sounds good to me," Justin said smoothly. "I have to be in London on Thursday anyway. The firm is handling a British-American publishing merger. This will save me another transatlantic flight."

"Two transatlantic flights," the countess corrected. "Good, that's settled, then."

Anne said nothing. She wondered at the air of happy anticipation on Justin's face. Was it for the prospect of a few days' vacation, or for Venice, or could any of it possibly be for spending some time alone with her? A flicker of hope flared inside her, then quickly died as another possibility occurred to her. Perhaps his enthusiastic expression was merely another piece of good acting for the countess's benefit.

- 16 -

"TELL THE DRIVER to go to my hotel first, Justin," the countess said imperiously after they'd finished lunch and Justin was ushering them into the taxi with his customary chivalry. "I could do with some beauty sleep, what with all those publicity photos coming up."

Anne was acutely conscious of Justin's leg pressed against hers as she sat wedged between him and the countess in the taxi's backseat. It's only that we're cramped for space, she told herself as his male warmth seeped through his brown silk slacks and her nylons and sent her pulses racing.

But when they dropped off the countess, he made no move toward the opposite side of the seat. His voice was warm and friendly as he said, "I want to talk to you, Anne. Would you like to come to my suite for a brandy?"

"Thank you. Brandy sounds very inviting," she said formally, trying not to let her hopes build. He probably wanted to discuss how to get out of going to Venice together, or perhaps suggest they go their separate ways when they arrived there.

It was only a few blocks from the countess's hotel to Justin's, and they rode in silence. As they entered the bustling lobby of the Grand Hotel, Anne noted how everyone from the doorman to the desk clerk to various bellhops greeted Justin by name and asked with more than perfunctory cordiality if he'd had a pleasant morning. On the elevator, too, several of the hotel guests spoke to him, and more than one woman glanced enviously at Anne before focusing wistful eyes on Justin.

His suite was as sumptuous as she'd remembered it. He seemed perfectly at ease in the luxurious surroundings as he escorted her across the Chinese rug to the dark-blue upholstered sofa.

"Those are stunning shoes," he commented. "But then, so is everything in your Marini wardrobe."

Had he noticed she was wearing the ankle bracelet? Anne longed to know, but she only said, "Oh, the shoes aren't Mario's. I brought them with me from New York."

"Really? I like them even better, then." He frowned. "Only kidding," he added hastily. "Make yourself comfortable while I get the drinks."

She watched as he strode to the bar and poured brandy into elegant crystal snifters. When he returned to the sofa and handed her one of the short-stemmed goblets, she held it to her nose and inhaled.

"I know I'm supposed to do this, but I feel a little silly," she confessed as he sat down next to her and draped his arm casually over the back of the sofa. Her heart was beating so loudly, she felt she had to talk or he would hear it. "This is the first time I've ever tried brandy, so I don't suppose I can properly appreciate it." Still, the sweet, peachlike aroma of the golden liquid made her feel pleasantly light-headed. Or was it Justin's nearness that made her feel this way?

"You're doing fine," he said easily. "Just take small sips. It's very potent stuff." He clinked his glass against hers and added lightly, "We've already drunk to the success of the Marini venture, so why don't we make this toast to Venice?"

"To Venice," Anne said, her heart hammering as she raised the goblet to her lips. She took a tentative sip and the brandy went down her throat with a burning sensation.

Justin sipped his brandy meditatively. "You know, Marie isn't exactly famous for lavish expense accounts," he remarked conversationally. "I get the idea this little holiday she's sending us on is for the purpose of fixing us up."

Anne took another swallow of her brandy and looked at him. If only she knew what thoughts lay behind those engimatic golden-brown eyes.

Justin set his glass on the walnut coffee table before them. "Maybe it's not such a bad idea—putting the honeymoon before the wedding, I mean."

The room seemed to dip and then swim before Anne's eyes, and she knew it wasn't the brandy. "Wedding?" she repeated foolishly, her hand trembling as she set her glass down next to Justin's.

"Our wedding," he said firmly. "I want to marry you, Anne. When Monica came out in that bridal gown and you started to cry, I suddenly realized what a fool I'd been. When you were so adamant about not living with me, I thought only that you didn't love me enough." He hesitated, then went on. "I have to be truthful. I've enjoyed my freedom, and, except for my student days with Clarissa, I'd never had any thoughts of marriage until I met you. Suddenly I discovered a traditional streak in myself. I wanted to settle down, raise a family. At first the revelation was frightening, and I resisted it."

"Are you sure it's what you want now, Justin?" Anne asked tremulously, too stunned to believe it could possibly be true. His proposal had filled her with a sweet radiance, but she had to be certain his whole heart was in it. There had been so much misunderstanding between them, and now this. . . . "That day at Hadrian's Villa . . ." she began.

"Don't remind me!" He raked his hands through his hair and looked at her beseechingly. "I never meant to insult you, Anne. When we were talking about answered prayers, I was going to ask you to marry me then, but...I don't know what happened. You and Chuck had decided on a probation period..."

"*He* decided on a probation period," she admitted softly.

"But I thought you wanted it that way too. I didn't want to risk being rejected, and somehow I couldn't get the words out. You were looking at me, I don't know, kind of warily, and I remembered how you'd told me at our first meeting that you wanted more out of life than a house to clean and children to raise. I do want children, but most of all I want you, Anne. And you won't have to do any cleaning. I have a housekeeper who keeps my co-op as neat as a pin. We can eat out every night—"

"Oh, but I like to cook. And I want children—" Suddenly she was bursting with laughter.

"Then it's yes?" he interrupted eagerly. "Say it, Anne. Say you'll marry me, darling. I won't take no for an answer."

"But—"

"No buts. You're wearing the bracelet I gave you— I saw it at the restaurant when you were coming back from the ladies' room. You wouldn't have worn it unless you still cared for me, would you?"

"I've never stopped caring for you, Justin," she said simply, earnestly.

"Then tell me you'll be my wife. Say the words..."

"Yes, Justin, I'll marry you." With a great sigh she nestled into his waiting arms and was engulfed by the sweet warmth of his embrace.

"Oh, Anne, I've waited for this for so long." He punctuated endearments with feather-light kisses on her hair and forehead.

"What do you mean you've waited so long?" she

teased. "We've only known each other for a few weeks."

"But the moment I met you it felt as if I'd known you all my life, an eternity."

"An eternity!" she cried with mock outrage. "Has knowing me been so awful that it's felt like an *eternity*?" She moved away from him and crossed her arms over her chest, pretending to be deeply hurt.

"Anne, don't be ridiculous," Justin chided, chuckling and turning her toward him. He planted light, teasing kisses all over her face and on her unresponsive lips. "It's been a lovely eternity here in the Eternal City, a heaven on earth, the culmination of all my dreams."

Anne remained stiff in his arms, though she had trouble controlling the smile that threatened to break out. She raised a skeptical eyebrow and opened her mouth to speak, but Justin took full advantage and captured her mouth with his. His tongue parted her lips with hot insistence while he caressed her breasts, waist, and hips with slow, mesmerizing strokes. All at once the game was over and Anne wound her arms around his neck in total abandon.

Some moments later they pulled reluctantly apart. Anne gave a long, contented sigh. "Justin, my darling," she said breathlessly, toying with the lapels of his jacket, "you won't always be able to sweet-talk me with your glib tongue, but I do suspect your other methods of persuasion will do quite nicely. Where were we?"

"Right about here," he answered, kissing her again.

After an even longer interval, they broke apart once more. "Justin, I believe in long engagements..." Anne warned him, trying to be practical though her body was on fire with love and longing.

"Not too long," he pleaded, planting a kiss on her earlobe. "At least let me put a diamond on your finger before I go to London."

"London? Oh, yes, your publishing merger," she recalled forlornly.

"I wish I didn't have to go, but maybe you can come with me. Marie might just decide it's a good time for you to visit Dragu London." His eyes twinkled like golden stars. "I have a confession to make."

She regarded him quizzically. Why was he chuckling? "Yes?"

"When you went to the ladies' room at lunch, I leveled with Marie. I told her I wanted to marry you but didn't want to stand in the way of your new opportunities as her international representative. I explained that I thought I could arrange to spend more time in the firm's New York office, and wondered if your travel schedule would have some flexibility. She took it from there."

"Justin Bradley!" Anne was appalled. "You mean it wasn't her own idea to play Cupid and send us off to Venice?"

"Venice was Marie's idea," he assured her, "but she didn't have to play Cupid. Haven't I told you I was smitten the very first time I saw you?"

"Are you sure it was *love* you were smitten with?" she teased fondly, running a seductive finger across his warm lips.

"I'm positive," he assured her, sending her a warming look. "I love you to the very depths of my soul, and I always will. Forever. But," he added as she placed her lips against his throat and ran a caressing palm down his shirtfront, "if you insist on doing that, I'll have to prove the depth of my love in a more convincing manner."

"Oh, yes," she breathed adoringly, "I think I need to be convinced."

As he brought his lips to hers and her arms went around his neck, time and place became suspended. They pledged their love in a way that transcended words . . . and convinced Anne thoroughly that she was now and forever the only object of Justin's most ardent devotion.

All of the above titles are per $1.75 per copy

Available at your local bookstore or return this form to:

SECOND CHANCE AT LOVE
Book Mailing Service
P.O. Box 690, Rockville Centre, NY 11571

Please send me the titles checked above. I enclose _____
Include $1.00 for postage and handling if one book is ordered; 50¢ per book for
two or more. California, Illinois, New York and Tennessee residents please add
sales tax.

NAME _____

ADDRESS _____

CITY _____ STATE/ZIP _____
(allow six weeks for delivery)   SK-41

_____ 06696-6 **THE FAMILIAR TOUCH #85** Lynn Lawrence

_____ 06697-4 **TWILIGHT EMBRACE #86** Jennifer Rose

_____ 06698-2 **QUEEN OF HEARTS #87** Lucia Curzon

_____ 06850-0 **PASSION'S SONG #88** Johanna Phillips

_____ 06851-9 **A MAN'S PERSUASION #89** Katherine Granger

_____ 06852-7 **FORBIDDEN RAPTURE #90** Kate Nevins

_____ 06853-5 **THIS WILD HEART #91** Margarett McKean

_____ 06854-3 **SPLENDID SAVAGE #92** Zandra Colt

_____ 06855-1 **THE EARL'S FANCY #93** Charlotte Hines

_____ 06858-6 **BREATHLESS DAWN #94** Susanna Collins

_____ 06859-4 **SWEET SURRENDER #95** Diana Mars

_____ 06860-8 **GUARDED MOMENTS #96** Lynn Fairfax

_____ 06861-6 **ECSTASY RECLAIMED #97** Brandy LaRue

_____ 06862-4 **THE WIND'S EMBRACE #98** Melinda Harris

_____ 06863-2 **THE FORGOTTEN BRIDE #99** Lillian Marsh

_____ 06864-0 **A PROMISE TO CHERISH #100** LaVyrle Spencer

_____ 06865-9 **GENTLE AWAKENING #101** Marianne Cole

_____ 06866-7 **BELOVED STRANGER #102** Michelle Roland

_____ 06867-5 **ENTHRALLED #103** Ann Cristy

_____ 06868-3 **TRIAL BY FIRE #104** Faye Morgan

_____ 06869-1 **DEFIANT MISTRESS #105** Anne Devon

_____ 06870-5 **RELENTLESS DESIRE #106** Sandra Brown

_____ 06871-3 **SCENES FROM THE HEART #107** Marie Charles

_____ 06872-1 **SPRING FEVER #108** Simone Hadary

_____ 06873-X **IN THE ARMS OF A STRANGER #109** Deborah Joyce

_____ 06874-8 **TAKEN BY STORM #110** Kay Robbins

_____ 06899-3 **THE ARDENT PROTECTOR #111** Amanda Kent

_____ 07200-1 **A LASTING TREASURE #112** Cally Hughes $1.95

_____ 07201-X **RESTLESS TIDES #113** Kelly Adams $1.95

_____ 07202-8 **MOONLIGHT PERSUASION #114** Sharon Stone $1.95

_____ 07203-6 **COME WINTER'S END #115** Claire Evans $1.95

_____ 07204-4 **LET PASSION SOAR #116** Sherry Carr $1.95

_____ 07205-2 **LONDON FROLIC #117 (Regency)** Josephine Janes $1.95

All of the above titles are $1.75 per copy except where noted

---

Available at your local bookstore or return this form to:

SECOND CHANCE AT LOVE
Book Mailing Service
P.O. Box 690, Rockville Centre, NY 11571

Please send me the titles checked above. I enclose _____
Include $1.00 for postage and handling if one book is ordered; 50¢ per book for
two or more. California, Illinois, New York and Tennessee residents please add
sales tax.

NAME _____

ADDRESS _____

CITY _____ STATE/ZIP _____

(allow six weeks for delivery)   SK-41

WHAT READERS SAY ABOUT
SECOND CHANCE AT LOVE BOOKS

"Your books are the greatest!"
—*M. N., Carteret, New Jersey**

"I have been reading romance novels for quite some time, but the SECOND CHANCE AT LOVE books are the most enjoyable."
—*P. R., Vicksburg, Mississippi**

"I enjoy SECOND CHANCE [AT LOVE] more than any books that I have read and I do read a lot."
—*J. R., Gretna, Louisiana**

"I really think your books are exceptional ... I read Harlequin and Silhouette and although I still like them, I'll buy your books over theirs. SECOND CHANCE [AT LOVE] is more interesting and holds your attention and imagination with a better story line ..."
—*J. W., Flagstaff, Arizona**

"I've read many romances, but yours take the 'cake'!"
—*D. H., Bloomsburg, Pennsylvania**

"Have waited ten years for *good* romance books. Now I have them."
—*M. P., Jacksonville, Florida**

*Names and addresses available upon request